PETER CORRIS is known as the 'godfather' of Australian crime fiction through his Cliff Hardy detective stories. He has written in many other areas, including a co-authored autobiography of the late Professor Fred Hollows, a history of boxing in Australia, spy novels, historical novels and a collection of short stories about golf (see www.petercorris. net). In 2009, Peter Corris was awarded the Ned Kelly Award for Best Fiction by the Crime Writers Association of Australia. He is married to writer Jean Bedford and has lived in Sydney for most of his life. They have three daughters and six grandsons.

The Cliff Hardy collection

PETER CORRIS

THE BLACK PRINCE

ALLEN&UNWIN

SYDNEY • MELBOURNE • AUCKLAND • LONDON

This edition published by Allen & Unwin in 2014
First published by Bantam Books, a division of Transworld Publishers, in 1998

Allen & Unwin
83 Alexander Street
Crows Nest NSW 2065
Australia
Phone: (61 2) 8425 0100
Email: info@allenandunwin.com
Web: www.allenandunwin.com

Cataloguing-in-Publication details are available
from the National Library of Australia
www.trove.nla.gov.au

ISBN 978 1 76011 017 8 (pbk)
ISBN 978 1 74343 804 6 (ebook)

Printed and bound in Australia by Griffin Press

MIX
Paper from
responsible sources
FSC® C009448

The paper in this book is FSC certified.
FSC promotes environmentally responsible,
socially beneficial and economically viable
management of the world's forests.

For Lincoln Webb, who introduced me to the benefits of weight training and, although he didn't know it at the time, gave me some of the material for this book

PART
ONE

1

I was lying on my back with my right leg up in the air, trying to get my hands to reach to my ankle. They wouldn't do it. Mid-calf at best.

'I call those executive hamstrings,' Wesley Scott said. 'Do you play any sport, Mr Hardy?'

'Cliff,' I said, still trying and failing. I switched legs. Worse. 'I play a bit of tennis.'

'How often? Ease up, Cliff, you'll hurt yourself.'

I relaxed. 'About once a month.'

'Warm up? Stretch before and after?'

'No.'

'Like I say, executive hamstrings. Get up and let's look this over.'

I got up creakingly. Wesley Scott was the proprietor and trainer at the Redgum Gymnasium and Fitness Centre in Norton Street, Leichhardt. He was a West Indian who'd been British and European body-building champion in the 1970s before marrying an Australian woman and migrating. He had African features, ebony skin, a shaved head and a body of iron.

Lately, my own body had been letting me down. I was tired at night and in a recent tussle with a thug who was trying to maim the man I was protecting, I had to resort to very dirty tactics to subdue him. He was getting the better of me before I eye-gouged him. I didn't like either feeling and I decided that I needed some toning up. Hence the visit to the gym for a 'fitness assessment'.

Wesley Scott had prodded and poked me, put me on an exercise bike and used calipers on various parts of my body. He'd entered his findings on a chart and was examining it now. He wore a black singlet, a red and silver tracksuit bottom with matching Nikes and leaned elegantly on an exercise bench. 'Hmm, not too bad for your age. Body fat to weight ratio okay, could be better. Aerobic fitness above average but not by much. Flexibility poor. You should be ashamed of yourself.'

I was unprepared for that and bridled a bit. 'Why? You said it wasn't too bad.'

'You're what? Let's see—184 centimetres, eighty-three kilos. I'd say you did a lot of sport when you were young, right?'

'Yeah. Surfing, boxing ... '

'Pretty good were you, man?'

'Not bad.'

'You had a naturally athletic physique and a strong constitution which you've let run down. When did you stop smoking?'

'Years ago.'

'Did it for how long?'

'Too long.'

'How much do you drink?'

'Too much.'

'What I mean. You go on as you are and you're going to tear a hamstring playing tennis or do a knee ligament. What kind of work do you do?'

'Security, that sort of thing.'

'Shit! Does that get physical?'

I thought of the heavy with the hard stomach and the knuckleduster. 'Occasionally. Not if I can help it.'

'So why are you here?'

His manner was a bit hard to take—almost aggressive, not quite. Very serious, but slightly mocking. He smiled, then threw a punch at me. From old habit, I slipped it and moved inside and could have thumped him over the heart except that I suspected it would have hurt me more than it would him.

'Hey, Cliff, you're quick. That's good.'

He was pleased and I was pleased. That got us on a better footing and I told him about the fight I'd almost lost and the tiredness and a few aches and pains stemming from old injuries.

'I can give you a weight training and stretching program that'll make a new man of you if you stick at it. Three days a week, an hour per session. Plus some deep tissue massage that'll hurt but get the kinks out.'

I signed up for five hundred dollars for a six-month program and started going to the gym early on Monday, Wednesday and Friday mornings. The first day, Clinton, Wesley's son, a slim coffee-coloured youth with cropped hair and perfect teeth doing a degree in human movement at the

Southwestern University, took me through the stretching exercises and showed me how to work the weight machines. Bench press, leg press, leg curls, pull-downs, back extensions, abdominal crunches and sessions on the exercise bike and rowing machine. Gradually, I upped the weights and the repetitions and was gratified to find myself getting stronger and more flexible.

To my surprise, I enjoyed the work-outs and the camaraderie among the people in the gym. No poseurs or narcissists, Wesley's clients were serious trainers—professional men and women, basketballers and footballers, police, dancers and actors of both sexes—a mixed bunch. When Wesley was on deck the radio played ABC Classic FM; when Clinton was in charge it was Triple J.

Wesley turned out to be a man of many parts. He'd been a jazz musician, a stage and TV actor and stuntman in Britain, a county cricketer and he held a Master's degree in Physical Education. He had a passion for Mozart and Shakespeare and was apt to quote from Bill when he was pummelling the hell out of me. His wife was a teacher. He had a daughter at the Conservatorium and he was active in Sydney's surprisingly large West Indian community. After a couple of months, having enjoyed his stories about London, the Portobello Road, Yul Brynner and other big names, and endured his Shakespearian allusions, I counted him as a friend.

Gyms, I found, are strange places. All the sweat and strain doesn't conceal subtle tensions that can lie under the surface. Workout partners can in fact be engaged in bitter competition; instructors can offend the clients with a misplaced word about technique and the instructors themselves can fall out. As far as I could see things weren't entirely harmonious between Wesley and Clinton. Clinton's attendance was somewhat irregular and he struck me as moody. Once, when he hadn't showed up for a spell I asked Wesley about him.

'In a huff,' he said. 'Pauline, his sister, said something to him about the way he treated women and he took it wrong. Well, he took it right, I guess. He's treated a few girls badly. He stormed off and said he'd never bring a girl home again.'

'That'll blow over when he wants a good feed.'

Wesley smiled without humour. 'He's a good boy, but he needs to learn something about reliability.'

'I'm still learning about that myself.'

'He takes things to heart. He's fought with everyone in the family at one time or another.'

I didn't put much store in that. So had I.

A week or so later I rolled in for my massage after upping the weights on the leg press and increasing the reps on the abdominal crunches. I pushed open the door to the massage room, feeling pretty pleased with myself, thinking of investing in new gym gear. The ancient tennis shorts were getting pretty ratty.

'Once more unto the breach, dear friends, once more,' I intoned. 'We'll stop the gap ... Hell, what's the matter, Wes?'

I'd expected to find Wesley flexing his muscles,

leering and slapping his oiled hands together with a sound like a thunderclap. But he was sitting, dressed as I'd never seen him, in jeans, shirt and leather shoes, in a chair in a corner of the room. He was forty-four and normally looked ten years younger; now he looked his age and a bit more. His massive shoulders were slumped and his usually taut, noble face was sagging.

'Hello, Cliff. You look cheerful.'

I eased into the room carefully. 'Compared to you, Tim Fischer'd look cheerful. What's up?'

He looked at me but he wasn't seeing me. His eyes were bloodshot and seemed to be focused on a point far beyond the walls around us. 'Clinton,' he said. 'We haven't seen or heard from him in three weeks, apart from one phone call to his mother. We don't know where the fuck he is.'

In our brief acquaintance I'd only known Wesley to swear a few times—when he was really amused, seriously angry or repeating what someone else had said. Now the swearing underlined his distress. I wiped my face with the towel I had hanging around my neck and draped it over my shoulders. I'd been expecting to be rubbed until I glowed. It wasn't going to happen and I didn't want to get too cool too quickly. I sat on the massage table and worked my arms. Dedicated trainers develop physical tics like boxers.

'Clinton doesn't live at home?'

Wesley shook his head. 'No, he moved out two years ago when he started university. He's lived in a few shared houses out that way—Campbelltown, Picton. You know, like students do. Most recently he was living in Helensburgh. But he kept in touch, sort of—phoned, came home for meals and to do his washing. He worked in here from time to time. Hell, when it suited him. You saw him in the gym. And he usually slept at home those nights. He didn't show up the week before last. Nothing new in that. I phoned and there was no answer. I thought what the hell, he's gone off with a team, forgot to tell us about it. Or there was a girl involved. He's always been a more or less steady lad but he loses his head over girls. And remember I told you about that business with his sister. I thought maybe he was making a point. I wasn't too worried. Next week no show and I phone again. The kid he shares the house with says he hasn't seen him for three weeks. He's pissed off about the rent. Shit!'

He banged his fist into his palm with a force that would've broken a brick. 'I should've gone down straightaway when he didn't turn up. Mandy wanted me to go but I was busy and she's over-protective. She can't drive for a bit after that whiplash she got a while back. I went yesterday.'

'Easy,' I said. 'What did you find when you got there?'

'Nothing, sweet f.a. His car's still there and all his clothes and other stuff as far as I could see. But he's . . . ' He broke off and rubbed at his eyes with his huge fists. If he'd been doing much of that it explained their bloodshot condition.

'So what did you do?'

'I told the police at Helensburgh. They went through all the motions but, you know how it is, a black kid goes missing. They don't give a fuck.'

'What about a girlfriend?'

'First thing I thought of, but that's it. He hasn't got one just now. Broke up with the last one nearly a year ago. Nice girl she was. I asked the kid in the house . . . Christ, I came on a bit heavy I suppose, and I didn't get anything out of him really. But he didn't mention a girl.'

'What about his friends at university?'

He looked up again and this time he was seeing me and what I was seeing was despair and guilt etched into his features and movements. 'He's twenty years old, Cliff. He's a man. You haven't got any kids, have you?'

I shook my head. When I hear about this sort of thing I'm not sorry about it.

'You don't know what it's like. You raise them from the time you can nearly hold them in your two hands.' He spread his fingers, showing huge pink palms. Wesley Scott was 190 centimetres plus, with hands to match. 'When they're young, you know all their friends. Shit, you're feeding them half the time. Then they grow up to be as big as you and you have to let them go. You don't know who their friends are any more. They don't come around on their fucking bikes. They've all got cars and you never see them. You're lucky if you get your own kid's new address and phone number inside a couple of weeks when he moves house. That's the way it is.'

I could imagine it and how hard it must be. But my professional instincts were taking over. *You can find out*, I thought. *But only if you know how.*

I had a raft of questions but it was more a moment for counselling. Without quite meaning it, I said things about how good the police were in these matters and how few adult males who dropped out of sight came to any harm. Wesley shook his head, flicking off these suggestions the way a dog shakes off water.

'Mandy's going out of her brain. I think she blames me in some way. Pauline can't practise or study and I can't think of a fucking thing to *do*!'

'I could look into it for you, Wes. I've got a private enquiry agent's licence. Might be able to help.'

He lifted his head and seemed to almost rise out of his seat as if reaching for a rung on a ladder. 'God,' he said. 'A private detective. I've been thinking of you as the ex-boxer security guard coming good again. You're a bloody private detective, are you? Would you take it on, Cliff? Please?'

2

Wesley Scott wasn't wealthy but he was prosperous. The gym fees weren't cheap and he had a full list of customers; he did private massages at hefty rates for some well-connected people, like judges and politicians; he was on the training staff of a pro basketball team and he was often called in as a consultant by other sporting organisations. He explained all this to me after I'd told him that my fees were two hundred dollars a day and expenses.

'I can afford you,' he said. 'And hiring you makes it feel like I'm doing something. Mandy'll feel the same.'

'I'd be happy to put in some time on it for friendship's sake.'

'No way! And now that you've given me the idea, if you don't agree I'll hire another detective.'

That was the clincher. I got what details I could—a copy of the missing person's report Wesley had lodged with the police, Clinton's address in Helensburgh, the name of the person he shared the house with, the make and colour of his car, something on the courses he was doing and a note from Wesley authorising me to inspect his son's belongings. I told Wesley I'd fax him a contract which he could sign and fax back. He insisted on writing out the retainer cheque there and then. I didn't protest; things do become more serious when money changes hands. I asked Wesley if he had a photograph. He rummaged in a drawer and came up with a recent snap taken by Mandy. She'd caught her boy standing with his arms in the air and a wide smile on his handsome face. He wore tight shorts and a sleeveless black jersey with a red diagonal stripe on it. I could see four goalposts in the background, two tall, two shorter.

'Australian football,' I said.

Wesley shrugged. 'The game's a mystery to me but the boy's good at it. He plays for Campbell-town in the local competition. Centre half-forward, whatever that means. I've watched him play. He kicks goals. He's just kicked one in the picture there. Strange game—they pass forward and back, no offside. Soccer's my game. You?'

'Union, used to be. I've lost interest lately.' I wiped my hands on the towel before picking up the cheque and the photo. 'What other sports does he play?'

'You name it. He's off a five handicap at golf, plays basketball for the university . . . '

'I get the idea. I'll start as soon as I get cleaned up. I'll put my numbers on the fax. Ring me anytime, especially if you hear from him. I hope you will.'

'Okay,' Wesley said, but the gloom was settling back on him.

'Look, Wes, is there anything you haven't told me? Any trouble he might have been in?'

He shook his head. 'That's part of the problem. I've been thinking about that, thinking back. But he never put a foot wrong. No joy-riding, pot-smoking, getting pissed. He doesn't drink or smoke. There's nothing, nothing at all.'

I patted him on the shoulder and headed off, but what he'd said worried me. I don't believe in paragons of virtue.

I drove home, cleaned up, went to the office and sent the fax. I tidied up a few loose ends and set off for Helensburgh. Not being a skier, I don't think winter shows off any place to advantage, and it's certainly not the best time to visit Helensburgh. The town, a mining and logging centre that also services some farms and orchards in the area, sits in the hills to the north of the Illawarra escarpment. In fine weather it might look picturesque from certain angles although it's basically just a well-treed suburb, but as I drove in it seemed to be huddled down under a thin mist as if getting ready to be rained on.

I located Hillcrest Street and drove slowly along it looking for the right number. The street could have crested a hill once, but the spread of houses, a couple of blocks of units, the bitumen, cement kerbing and guttering and lines of lampposts along the major streets had obliterated the original topography. A few residents had left decent sized gum trees and wattles on their blocks, but most had embraced the shrub, the hedge, the lawn and the flower bed.

Clinton Scott's house was a standard post-World War II fibro box with an iron roof, skimpy front porch and small windows. The slight lurch to the left of the whole structure suggested decayed stumps; the broken-down fence and overgrown garden shrieked cheap rent. I parked and walked through a gate wide enough to admit a car. It was held open by a brick. Tyre tracks showed where a car or cars had been parked but there weren't any in evidence. The front yard was scruffy, although efforts had been made. At a guess, the grass had been cut roughly with a hand mower fairly recently and some of the more aggressive weeds and thistles had been pulled up and put in a heap.

The mist was thickening towards rain as I walked up the gravel path to the front of the house. I knocked, got no response and tried the door. It opened and I went in, making as much noise as I could. There was a threadbare carpet runner down the passage on top of linoleum. It was a lino kind of house. A bedroom off each side of the passage; a kitchen-cum-sitting room after that with a bathroom and toilet off to one side. The back porch ran the width of the house and had been built in with masonite lining and louvre windows. Everything was very basic—the plumbing, the two-bar radiators, the small television, the portable CD player—but the place was clean and tidy. A few cups, plates and dishes had been washed and stacked in a plastic rack to dry; a pedal bin in the kitchen was lined with newspaper and there were two spare rolls in the toilet.

It was easy to tell which bedroom was Clinton's—golf clubs, a squash racket, battered size 12 Reeboks. The books on the shelves were about anatomy, pharmacology and physiology as well as sporting biographies, a few paperback novels and a history of Australian football. A poster on the back of his door showed a huge man in a red and white jersey flying high over a pack of other players to catch a football. It was signed in thick Texta colour 'Best wishes, Clint—Plugger'. Like Wesley, I didn't understand Aussie Rules, but you couldn't live in Sydney in the last few years without hearing about Tony Lockett.

I turned the room over thoroughly and became convinced that Clinton had either left voluntarily—no wallet, some empty clothes hangers, no socks or underwear, a docket for a new pair of sneakers but no sign of them, no carryall—or someone had tried very hard to make it look that way. The room was tidy, but not unnaturally so. His university notes, neatly enclosed in labelled folders, were on the small table that served as his study desk. I flicked through them but it was all gibberish to me. There were three essays in a drawer, one for each of his subjects. He'd got two A−s and a B+. Academic failure wasn't his problem. Not much in that to reassure Wesley.

I searched all the obvious hiding places, tapped for loose floorboards, found nothing. The bathroom, clean like the kitchen, was minimally equipped on first inspection—one of everything only. A closer look showed that a few things like goanna oil, tinea cream and elastic bandages had been tucked away in a cupboard. At a guess, the other kid in the house had done that. The cabinet that held the mirror had been moved up thirty centimetres from its original position. I remembered that Clinton was almost as tall as his father. The old holes had been neatly filled and painted over. Good kid.

'Where the hell are you, Clinton?' I said out loud.

I left the bathroom and was about to go into the other bedroom when I heard a noise outside. A car pulling up. I went into Clinton's room and looked through the window. A light blue Holden Commodore pulled up beside the house, windscreen wipers working against the heavy rain. A tall, thin young man got out, deposited a couple of plastic shopping bags on the ground, and strode quickly back to the gate. He kicked the brick aside and closed it. He wore jeans, a bomber jacket and boots. His black hair was long and lank and he flicked it back with a toss of his head as he headed for the porch.

He opened the door and I stepped out into the passage. He dropped one of the bags and I heard glass break.

'What . . . who're you?'

I moved forward. 'More to the point, what're you doing driving around in Clinton Scott's car?'

For a young person who'd had a considerable shock he showed a good deal of poise. He took a step and lowered the other bag to the floor before closing the door behind him. He stared at me and flicked back the hair again to get a better look. I did my best not to look threatening and he evidently decided that he wasn't in danger from me because the stiffness went out of him.

'I can explain that,' he said. 'Can you explain what you're doing here?'

I admired his cool. I moved to one side. 'That's a fair enough question. Let's go and sit down and talk. I could do with a cup of coffee.'

He didn't look pleased but he nodded and lifted the bags gingerly. We went through to the kitchen and he put the shopping on the table. He lifted out the contents, tinned food mostly, and groaned when a can of baked beans came out covered in dripping thick red fluid. 'Shit, the tomato sauce's busted.'

'Sorry,' I said. I opened out the other bag and freed two bottles of cheap red wine. 'Better that than the plonk.'

He grinned. 'Yeah. You're right. Hang on, I'll just clean this up a bit and put the kettle on.' He shrugged off his jacket and put it neatly on the back of a chair. He went about the business of wiping the tomato sauce off tins and packets and stowing them calmly and efficiently in a cupboard. I sat and watched him, thinking how unusual this was. When you enter a house illegally and surprise the occupant you don't normally encounter a polite and competent young person who makes you feel rather clumsy. He filled an electric kettle, plugged it in and spooned instant coffee into two mugs. He got milk from the fridge and set it beside the mugs.

'Sugar?'

'No,' I said, almost rudely. Unusual circumstances are all very well, but I didn't want this to turn into a tea party. I opened my notebook and looked at the notes I'd taken on what Wesley had told me. 'You're Noel Kidman, is that right?'

That startled him. 'I thought you were a friend of Clint's or something, not a policeman.'

'You were right the first time.'

The jug boiled. He made the coffee and brought it to the table. He sat down and fussily rearranged his jacket on the chair. 'Clint hasn't paid any rent for four weeks. I've had to pay the last two lots myself. It's been hard. I felt justified in using his car to save on fares. And I suppose because I'm pissed off with him.'

'Okay.' I passed one of my cards across the table and took a sip of the coffee. 'I've been hired by Clinton's father to find him. This is the obvious starting place. Have the police talked to you?'

'No. There was a cop car here yesterday when I was coming home but I waited until it went away.'

'Why?'

'I don't trust the police.'

'I see. I understand you saw Mr Scott a couple of days ago?'

'That's right. He was very aggressive.'

'He's upset.'

He drank some coffee. 'Well, so am I bloody upset. I'm in my final year. I've only got three units to get but they're bloody hard. Plus I'm doing two part-time jobs. It's tough. The rent here's cheap and I can't afford to move, but I can't afford to pay it all myself. I'll have to get someone else in and that's not easy at this time of year. Clinton's left me in the fucking lurch.'

'I sympathise,' I said. 'But he's missing. It's not just that he's pissed off somewhere. Something might have happened to him. Doesn't that affect how you feel?'

It was clear from the defiant way he looked and drank more coffee that it did, but he wasn't going to admit it. 'Shit, what could happen to him? He's as tough as they come, super fit. The Black Prince, that's what they call him. He's on top of every- thing. Well, he was . . . '

'Okay, Noel, now we're getting to it. He was on top of everything until when?'

He rubbed his chin where dark bristles were beginning to show through the pale skin. He was thinner than he should have been and his eyes showed tiredness and strain. 'All right, about a month ago he went into a bit of a spin. I thought it was about this girl he had . . . '

'You didn't mention a girl to his father.'

'I was scared of him. I thought he was going to take the place apart. I said as little as I possibly could.'

I nodded. I could imagine an upset Wesley being very frightening. 'A girl.'

'Yeah, well, Clinton seemed dead keen on her, then she was out of the picture. I've known him for a couple of years and he's had more girls than I've had hot dinners. I thought he'd get over it but he didn't seem to. He got moody and that. He stopped going to football and basketball training, or turned up late. He got sloppy around the house and hard to get on with. He was like a different person.'

'What was her name?'

'Don't know.'

'Come on, he must've called her something. What about when they talked on the phone?'

He rubbed at the stubble. 'I suppose so, but I can't remember. It didn't go on for that long, only a couple of weeks, and I never met her. He never brought her here the way he did the others. All I know is she was at the uni and she played basketball. That's how he met her. I suppose I should have been more sympathetic when he told me, but I've got my own worries, what with the essays and trying to work and get enough fucking sleep to be able to think straight . . . '

'When he told you what?'

'That she was dead.'

3

Noel Kidman was studying computer science and had a job lined up with a company setting up web sites for businesses. It was a big opportunity in a competitive field and he needed his degree to clinch it. The need dominated his thinking and blunted his human responses. We talked some more over the coffee and he admitted as much and felt guilty about it. He was bright but under a lot of pressure and Clinton's defection threatened to be a last straw. With absolutely no authority to do so, I told him to continue to use the car and that I'd get Clinton's father to pay the back rent and pay for at least the next month.

'D'you mean that?' He looked as if a sack of cement had just been lifted off his shoulders.

'Sure. And you phone me if you remember anything that might be helpful.'

He fingered my card. 'I will. Shit, d'you really think . . . I mean, foul play?'

'I always think foul play in my game,' I said. 'That way I get a pleasant surprise every once in a while.'

'That sounds depressing.'

'It has its moments. What's the phone number here?'

'It's disconnected. I mean, it stopped working and I can't afford to pay for it anyway.'

'Since when?'

He thought about it. 'Since just after Clint's Dad rang.'

All that gave me something to chew on but it didn't taste good. On the drive to Campbelltown where the main campus of the university was located, I tried to remember what Clinton had been like. Not much stuck in my mind apart from his athleticism and patience with someone in an early stage of decay. Wesley had said the boy had never given him much trouble and certainly hadn't hinted at mental instability. There was nothing in his background or lifestyle to suggest that. Still, there was the business of his multiple girlfriends, then a serious if somewhat mysterious relationship ending on the woman's death. Worrying.

I forced myself to stop thinking about the matter while I negotiated the unfamiliar roads in the rain being driven by a gusty wind. One minute the wipers were working overtime, the next it was only a drizzle, then it became fierce again. Difficult conditions and all the other drivers were taking it slow. It was going to be late on a bad afternoon when I arrived—not the best time to be asking questions about a young woman who'd recently died. But there's no good time for something like that.

I'm not often in Campbelltown, which tends to be serviced for my line of work from Parramatta, and I'd never been to the Southwestern University. The campus was a kilometre from the centre of the town, a collection of low-rise, cement block buildings scattered over what had probably once been orchards or market gardens. I found the campus map, located the sports centre and parked in the visitors' area. In a small set-up like this, it wasn't so far from the sports centre. In the bigger universities it either doesn't exist or is a bus ride from the action. I was wearing jeans and a leather jacket. I exchanged the jacket for a hooded parka and ran through the rain to where the lights had been turned on against the late afternoon gloom.

The building was warm and bright, very welcome after the nastiness outside. An impossibly healthy-looking woman wearing a tracksuit with the name Kathy printed on the top was dealing with business at the reception desk. I shook water from my parka, taking care that it fell outside the door, made sure my shirt was tucked in and approached the desk. I could hear squash being played somewhere, an aerobics instructor screaming her directions and the unmistakable sound of basketball players pounding the boards. The average age of everyone in the place was probably twenty-one, but hell, I was bench-pressing quite a few kilos myself these days.

'Can I help you, sir?' Kathy said.

'Hello. Do you know a young man named Clinton Scott?'

'Clint, yes. He plays basketball for . . . '

I held up my PEA licence. 'He's missing. Has been for some time. I've been hired by his father to find him.'

'Missing. Gee, I don't know. Yes, I guess I haven't seen him here for a while but I thought he might be injured or something. That happens all the time and they go off for physio and rehab and that. Missing, what . . . ?'

'There could be explanations, all sorts of explanations. But I've been told that he had a girlfriend who also played basketball and that she died. Do you know anything about that?'

She shook her head. 'No. I haven't heard anything like that. Who was she?'

'I don't know the name.' The thought struck me then that Clinton might not have been telling the truth to Noel and that this might be a dead end.

'I play soccer,' Kathy said. 'I don't know much about the basketballers, the women that is. You should talk to Tanya. She's the basketball coach. She'd know.'

'Tanya?'

'Tanya Martyn. With a "y". She coaches basketball, hockey, and track and field. I think she's here tonight.' She consulted a chart on the wall. Her own name was slotted into a board showing who was on duty at the desk—Katharine Simpson.

'Yeah, she should be finishing up with the hockey people in twenty minutes. I can send her a message that you want to see her if you like.'

'Please.' I handed her a card and she tapped away on a keyboard. She made to return the card but I told her to keep it and to mention my enquiry to anyone she thought might be able to help. My guess was that this was the listening post for the sporting fraternity of the campus, and that there would be no better broadcaster than Kathy Simpson.

'Mr Hardy is it?'

I'd wandered off to watch a squash game from above the court. I've never enjoyed squash but I admire the stamina of the players. I spun around to see a tall, dark woman in a blue tracksuit examining me. She had a clipboard in her hand and gave the impression that she was going to give me marks for cleanliness and posture.

'Ms Martyn. Yes, I'm Hardy. I wonder if I can have a few words with you. Has Kathy told you about my enquiry?'

She drew nearer and dropped the clipboard onto a chair. She had short hair, fine features and a light film of sweat on her face. 'Yes,' she said. 'But you've got things screwed up.'

'How's that?'

'I'm sitting down. I'm beat.'

We sat in the chairs with our backs to where the pair below where beating hell out of the little black ball.

'I suppose you *look* like a private eye. Big enough. Tough. Could I see some ID and something to prove you're doing what you say you are?'

I showed her my licence and hesitated, then I remembered Wesley Scott's note. I hadn't had to show it to Noel Kidman. I showed it to Tanya Martyn.

She took a slim glasses case out of her pants pocket, put on the half-glasses and read the note. She was in her thirties, I guessed, young to need reading glasses, but you can never tell when things are going to break down. She took the glasses off and put them away. 'Okay. Looks kosher.'

'You're careful.'

'Have to be.'

'What d'you mean?'

'Think about it. I'm working with young people. Hands-on stuff, as it were. Think about the harassment and abuse possibilities.'

'Come on.'

'It's true, same with giving out information. Tricky. Anyway, what's happened to Clint Scott?'

'Hold on. I'm supposed to be asking the questions.'

The thwack of the squash ball seemed to underline her clipped delivery. 'Me first.'

'He hasn't been seen by friends or family for going on a month. I haven't checked with his academic and sports people here yet, but I think it'll be the same story with them. His family's worried. The police are doing what they do.'

She nodded. 'Black—therefore, unpredictable. Not important.'

I shrugged. 'You could say that. I'm a friend of the father. I work out at his gym. Clinton taught me the ropes. I . . . '

'No need to be defensive, Mr Hardy. I'll tell you what I know.'

It was getting on for six o'clock. I was tired and in need of a drink. It's easy to get testy under those circumstances and blow an interview, especially with someone who clearly had her own agenda like Ms Martyn. I ignored the reproach and tried to look obliging.

'I know Clinton Scott, of course. Good athlete, very good. Bit predatory with the women they tell me. He and Angela Cousins had a thing going for a while, but she's not dead. Better if she was, probably.'

'Could you explain that?'

'I'm not sure that I should.'

'Why not?'

'Private detectives. They're always in the media, talking on television . . . '

'Not me. I take the private part seriously. And I'm a friend of this kid's father. I'm not interested in anything but finding him. Believe me.'

She sighed. 'You're convincing. Angela played guard for the team here. Tall kid, 180 plus. Bloody good, but lightly built. Aboriginal ancestry.'

'Yes.'

'Not so's you'd notice. White as me, whiter, but she was proud of it and why not? Anyway, she took a wrong turning.'

'Meaning?'

She moved closer to me, so close I could feel the warmth of her. She must've felt my warmth, too, and she didn't move away. Her voice went low, conspiratorial. 'She got on the steroids somehow and was given some bad stuff or had a bad reaction. Look, this has all been kept very quiet after the stuff about the League players. I shouldn't be telling you . . . '

'It's all right. It goes no further.'

'It was kept quiet partly on account of her family, partly because it's the last thing the university needs. Funding and that. I don't pretend it's altruistic. I only know about it because ... well, I knew the signs.'

'So how is she?'

'She's in a coma. Has been for a couple of weeks. Hopeless. It's only a matter of time till they pull the plug.'

4

Tanya Martyn gave me the address of Angela
Cousins' parents in Parramatta. Angela herself was
on life support in the Parramatta District Hospital
and Ms Martyn's understanding was that her case
came up for review by the medical authorities
very soon. I made notes and she jiggled her car
keys indicating that I didn't have much longer.

'Thank you, Ms Martyn, you've been very
helpful.'

Somehow we'd drawn closer so that we were
almost touching. Now she drew away a bit as if
she'd just noticed. 'Can't see how.'

'One last thing—is there anyone who might
know something about what was going on in
Clinton's head? The kid he shares a house with
doesn't know anything and he's been out of touch
with his family.'

She stood up and flexed her shoulders, picked
up the clipboard. We moved towards the door.
It was raining hard outside and the sight of it
seemed to affect her. 'I hate the rain,' she said.
'Silly but I do. I should live in San Diego where
it doesn't happen. Sorry, what was that you said?'

'Someone who knew Clinton intimately.'

She laughed harshly. 'Yeah, well, you could try Ted Kinnear. Coaches the men's basketball team. Coach is supposed to know what the players are up to. Hah. Look at me—at first I thought Angela was bulking up from the weights. Still, worth a try. You'd get him here tomorrow morning.'

'Thanks.'

She turned away and then turned quickly back, shaking her head. 'Hold on. Ted Kinnear handed over to his assistant recently. Leo Carey's the man you want.'

I thanked her yet again. She nodded and strode out into the rain as if daring it to trouble her. I felt oddly lonely after she'd gone. That's been happening to me lately. I get a feeling with someone that a connection's possible here, and then it falls away.

I sat damply in my car thinking about what I'd got. It seemed like quite a haul of information for comparatively little investment of time, but which way did it point? I was going to have to stay in the district to talk to the basketball coach the next day so I decided to put in one more house call. In any case, Parramatta would be a better place to stay in than Campbelltown—better chance of a decent meal at least.

I caught the tail end of 'PM' as I drove to Parramatta. Pauline Hanson's popularity was rising rapidly according to the polls, as people saw in One Nation a way to show how pissed off they were with the others. Bad news. But the rain eased. I found the Cousins' address in the northern section of the town, across the street from the Pentecostal church. As always when confronting Aborigines, I had to prepare myself. *Don't patronise; don't be too matey; don't* ... I'd soldiered with Aborigines, boxed with them, drunk with them, joked with them for more than twenty years and still I never felt comfortable at first meetings. My English, Irish gypsy and French ancestors had arrived in the late nineteenth century and lived in cities. I had no reason to feel personally guilty about the dispossession of the Aborigines but I did.

I exchanged my damp parka for my dry leather jacket, smoothed my hair and straightened my shirt collar after doing up two more buttons. There were lights on in the house, an unremarkable double-fronted brick-veneer job with a neat front garden and a cement path. I pushed open the wrought-iron gate and stopped dead still. The dog occupying the middle of the path was low-slung, black and emitting a barely suppressed fury. It barked three times and I didn't move a muscle. It looked like a Staffordshire terrier, normally a congenial breed, but all terriers can bite and hold ferociously and you never can tell.

An outside light came on over the front door. It opened and a tall man stood there.

'Who's that?'

'Are you Mr Cousins?'

'I am. Who're you?'

I told him, keeping my voice down, no need to

advertise the business to the neighbours. 'Would you call off the dog, please?'

'Jerry, back here!'

The dog retreated and I advanced a few steps, brushing away a branch of a shrub that had partly obscured my vision of the man. I could now see that he was tall, thin and straight, with brown skin and a frizz of white hair. I stopped short of the porch but put one foot up on it.

'Hardy,' he said. 'Private detective. You the bloke Jimmy Sunday talks about?'

Some time back I'd helped ex-fighter Jimmy Sunday straighten a few things out for Jacko Moody, who was then on his way to the national middle-weight title. 'I know Jimmy. Yes, I guess so.'

'Come in, then. Don't worry about the dog, he won't hurt you.'

'He puts on a good act.'

'That's all it is.' He reached out and we shook hands. It was like touching wood; I felt thickened knuckles and callused fingers and palm—a boxer and an axeman for sure.

We went into the smallish house which was similar in design to the one in Helensburgh but in much better condition. Cousins led me into the sitting room and turned off the TV set. He gestured for me to sit down and I took a chair near the fire and leaned forward to rub my hands in front of it.

Cousins smiled. 'They used to say you'd get chilblains from doing that. I never did. Tell you the truth, I don't know what a chilblain is. What can I do for you, Mr Hardy?'

'I'm looking for young Clinton Scott. He's dropped out of sight and his family's worried. I've been told he kept company with your daughter. I'm sorry, I know what happened to her and I know this must be hard for you, but I thought you might be able to help me.'

I guessed his age at forty-plus and they hadn't been easy years. A few of the marks of boxing were on his face—a little scar tissue around the eyes, a flattened and marginally off-centre nose, one slightly thickened ear—but the lines and planes of his face suggested that his usual expression was one of peace and good humour. There was an uppishness to him. At the mention of Angela, some of this fell away.

'I don't know,' he said. 'I thought you might be here about the old-time boxers' association, something like that. You've got the look yourself . . . '

'No, sorry. Not that.'

All my worries about the barriers of ethnicity fell away. This was a man in pain and I'd dealt with plenty of those. 'I knew a Joey Cousins once,' I said. 'I boxed with him in the army. He was a sergeant. Welterweight. Good punch.'

Cousins brightened a little and nodded. 'My uncle. I was named after him, but my dad was against fighting so I went under the name of Joey Lewis. Sort of joke, you know?'

'I get it. How did you do?'

He shrugged. 'West Australian middleweight title. Fought in the west mostly. Got to Adelaide a couple of times. Darwin. Never had the name to get fights in the east. I came east in the late seventies but the game was in the doldrums. Before Fenech and them. I had a few goes in the tents and that was enough for me. Gave it away.'

'Probably wise.'

'Yeah. I did all right. Worked in the timber game until that all slowed down. Got a fair package.'

I nodded. We'd covered some neutral ground now and made some connections. He cracked his knuckles and stared at the fire. 'Well, something to do with Angie?'

I gave him the story in as much detail as I could. He listened, still looking at the fire. The dog padded in from somewhere and curled up in front of the fire, not far from my feet. Cousins reached forward and patted him. The dog didn't stir.

'My wife's at her church group,' Cousins said. 'Got very churchy lately. Always a bit that way. Not a bad thing in a woman. Does no bloody good for me though. Fancy a drink?'

'That'd be good.'

He went out and came back with a longneck of VB and two glasses. He poured the drinks and took a judicious sip. 'Be easy to get on the piss after all this,' he said. 'But I won't. Wife needs me. Gotta slog on, haven't you?'

'Right.' I drank to that.

'Yeah. Well, Clinton. Bloody nice kid. Angie brought him around a couple of times. We both liked him. I've known a few West Indians here and there. Good people. I remember Julie, that's the wife, saying that it was a good combination,

West Indian and Koori. You know the Saunders family, Reg and them? Reg had a West Indian in the line, grandfather I think. And he was a captain in the army. First Koori officer. His kids've done well, too. My Julie was looking ahead ... See, Angie's our only kid and Julie comes from this big family down Bingara way, on the south coast. She's a Roberts, big mob of them down there. That's where we met. I mean, she's real light-skinned and the welfare took her away as a nipper and stuck her in an institution. She only connected up with her people much later. So it's all very important to her, like. She was thinking about grandchildren.'

He got up and opened a drawer in a dresser. He took out a framed studio photograph and showed it to me. Julie Cousins was many shades lighter than her husband and Angela was the same. They were a good-looking threesome, making allowances for Joe Cousins' hard knocks. Angela, who looked to be in her late teens, was tall and slight with an athletic carriage and a winning smile. Just looking at her image it was hard to believe that she wouldn't go on to do great things. In my jacket pocket I had the photograph of Clinton after kicking his goal—similarly promising and future problematical. I handed the picture back and he put it away.

'Did you see Clinton after Angela went into hospital?'

He nodded and drank some more beer. 'A couple of times. He was really cut up. Angry as hell. I went in one time and found him after he'd been to see her. He was crying and he was pulling his boot to bits.'

'What?'

'A footy boot. He had a sports bag with his gear in it. He'd taken out one of his boots and was ripping it to shreds with his hands. Not easy to do, that.'

'What did he have to say?'

'Not much. He'd been drinking pretty heavily I'd say. He nearly got run in by the cops, too.'

'How's that?'

'This was another time. Bit later. He was here. He'd brought us back from the hospital in his car. A copper came to talk to us, you know, about the steroids. It was the first Clinton had heard of it. Julie and me'd only been told the day before. We thought she'd had some sort of attack. Shit!'

He finished his drink and I followed suit. He refilled the glasses and it was as if we were drinking to lost hopes and broken dreams.

'What did Clinton do?'

'When the copper mentioned the steroids and asked us if we knew where Angie'd got them, Clinton went wild. We knew bugger-all, of course. Clinton screamed that it was impossible. That Angie wouldn't do anything like that. That's what I thought at first, but they explained the tests and all and you couldn't knock it. Clinton attacked the copper. I hauled him off and we got it calmed down, but he was off his head and it was touch and go for a bit, believe you me.'

That seemed to head off my next question— did Clinton know anything about how Angela made this fatal turning? Joe Cousins nursed his beer, turning the glass in his battered hands.

'There's no hope for her, you know,' he said. 'She's going soon. Julie's just getting her strength up for it. It's hard. It's fuckin' hard. I was disappointed in Clinton if you want to know the truth.'

'Why?'

He looked at me. His eyes were moist and he rubbed at them in much the same way as Wesley Scott had done. 'The last night we saw him, after a hospital visit, he said he'd get the people that gave Angie the steroids. He said he'd destroy them. But that's weeks ago. Julie wanted to talk to him, explain what was going to happen. Talk about a service or something. But his phone doesn't answer and it was no good leaving messages at the university. We haven't seen or heard from him since that night.'

'I'm sorry for your trouble,' I said. 'And I'm sorry to have had to bring all this up.'

He shook his head. 'It's all right. Better to talk than sit and brood about it. D'you reckon he meant it, about getting the bastard who gave her the steroids?'

'I think he did.'

'Good luck to him. I wish I could be there when he does.'

So do I, I thought.

5

Two glasses of beer on an empty stomach was an effective appetiser. I drove to the nearest motel, booked in and found a restaurant that served steak and salad and house wine for a reasonable price. It'd go on Wes Scott's bill but I never liked to pad the expenses for a friend. The food was good and the red must have been out of one of the better casks because it slid down nicely. The rain had stopped and the sky was clear. The air was cold, moved about by a slight breeze. After a day of driving and sitting I felt the need for exercise. I zipped up the leather jacket and walked around the town for an hour, deliberately keeping my mind off the case.

Parramatta has a real and honest feel to it, like a place that belongs where it is for real historical and geographical reasons, and does a job it's supposed to do. Like a lot of Australians, I feel a bit anxious when I'm a long way from the water, but Parramatta didn't set up too much of that, maybe because the river isn't far away and it leads to the harbour. Wednesday was evidently a quiet night in the centre. There were pubs doing reasonable business and the usual ebb and flow out of the takeaway joints, but no energy. That suited me. I was tired and my warm room with the double bed and an instant coffee with a dash of Johnny Walker red from the minibar was beckoning.

Back at the motel, I had a shower, wrapped the towel around me and did some stretching and a few push-ups. Nothing strenuous. I debated whether to have the laced coffee before, after or during making a report to Wesley. I decided on after and phoned him.

'Cliff, I was hoping you'd call.'

'Any news your end?'

'No. Nothing. What've you found out?'

They're often like that; the anxiety makes them unreasonable so that they think one day on the job should bring concrete results. It never does. I told Wesley about meeting Noel Kidman and the deal I'd made with him.

'That's fine. I'll send him a cheque. What else?'

'Nothing much, Wes. But there *was* a girl Clinton was involved with.' I described Angela Cousins. There was a silence so long I had to ask if he was still there.

'Yeah, I'm here. An Aboriginal girl? Why didn't he talk about her, or bring her home?'

'I think you know the answer to that.'

'God, I didn't think it was that serious.'

'Easy, Wes. I don't know the finer details of your family set-up.'

He managed a short laugh. 'You could hardly accuse Mandy of being prejudiced against blacks. No, I can't think of anything apart from the blue with Pauline. I'm beginning to wonder if I knew the boy at all.'

Joe Cousins was probably having the same thoughts, but at least the Scotts didn't have all their eggs in the one basket. I told Wesley what had happened to Angela and about Clinton's reaction. I didn't mention the drinking or the boot-shredding.

'Steroids? My god, Clinton really was hot on that subject. I told him I'd never taken them back in my body-building days. I had a hard time convincing him. He once said he was ashamed to be of the same race as Ben Johnson. I'm not surprised he went wild. The girl couldn't have done anything worse in his eyes.'

'She couldn't have done anything worse, period.'

'Of course. That's very sad. You say she's going to die?'

'Soon. It looks as if Clinton cut himself off from the girl's family as well as his own. They seem to have got on very well before that.'

A silence again while he absorbed the information that his son had been close to people he had chosen to keep separate from his family. When he spoke there was hurt and mystification in his voice. 'A few years back Clinton had a mate who got leukaemia. Clint was a tower of strength to that family—nothing he wouldn't do. I don't understand this. I don't understand anything. Why he wouldn't tell us about the girl. Why he'd cut off from her people. What d'you make of it?'

'It's too soon to say. I'm talking to Clinton's

basketball coach tomorrow. He might have some ideas. I should see Angela's mother too, for the woman's perspective. Can't say I'm looking forward to that.'

'Is there anything I can do, Cliff?'

'No. How are Mandy and Pauline bearing up?'

'It helped when I told them I'd hired you. I thought it would. We're counting on you, man.'

Just what you want to hear when all you've got is a few unconnected threads and some worrying suspicions. I didn't know anything about the emotional storms children can stir up or how adults cope with them. Maybe you need to be married with three kids to understand how life really is. If so, I'd missed the bus all along the line. I didn't know anything about the trade in steroids, but if it was a big money business then an angry kid blundering in could come to serious harm. I didn't admit any of this to Wesley. I told him I'd stay in touch. Then I made my drink and went to bed.

I carry shaving tackle, a toothbrush and a change of shirt in the car so I was able to scrub up reasonably well the next morning. I had orange juice and a packet of nuts from the minibar along with two cups of coffee for breakfast, paid my bill and headed back to the university. I passed the hospital on the way and thought about the young woman lying there with machines keeping her alive, technically. She evidently knew nothing about what had happened and was most likely already at peace. But she was leaving a lot of pain and distress behind her.

Leo Carey was in the middle of a coaching session with his players when I arrived. I sat at the side of the court and watched them going through the set plays, off-fence and de-fence as the language is, dribbling and practising all the other skills of the game. I used to play it at the Police Boys' Club when the hoop seemed to be halfway to the roof. The giants in this squad slam-dunked and took rebounds in the stratosphere.

The coach moved restlessly up and down the sideline, shouting and punching the air with his fist. Occasional collisions seemed to inspire him to greater fury and I couldn't tell whether he was glad his players were bumping the shit out of each other or deploring it. He was a tallish man in his forties, bald with the beginnings of a belly but with the old athlete's lightness of step. He wore a tracksuit and sneakers and looked as if he spent his entire life dressed like that. A stray ball bounced towards him and he scooped it up and returned it like a rocket while still bellowing.

The session ended and Carey despatched the various players to further tortures in the gym and pool and on the running track. He'd noticed me watching and came over to me when he'd completed his tasks.

'You a spotter?' he barked.

I was puzzled. 'What?'

'Talent spotter. Looking over my boys.'

'No, nothing like that.' I produced my credentials. 'I want to talk to you about Clinton Scott.'

The name seemed to take the aggression out of him. He slumped down on a seat in the row in front of me and stared at the court. 'Lost three out of four since he went missing.'

'He was good then?'

'Bloody good and could've been better if he wasn't so flaky and if he'd give that fuckin' ping-pong football away. Surefire way to do your knees, that game.'

'Flaky?'

Carey shrugged. 'Not the most regular at training. Missed a game when it suited him. Kinnear told me to give him plenty of rope so I did. Too much, maybe. The other boys didn't like it much.'

'Have you got any idea where he might have gone?'

He swivelled round to look at me. For a moment it seemed he wanted to say something, then he shook his head. 'No.'

'I know about Angie Cousins.'

'What d'you know?'

'That she was on steroids.'

'Is that so?'

'Come on. I know it's not widely known and I'm not going to broadcast it. I'm just interested in so far as it concerns Clinton. Look, I talked to Angie's father last night. You can call him and confirm that if you like.'

'No, I'll take your word for it. Shit of a thing, that. I once saw the two of them playing a bit of one-on-one. Sheer poetry. That's the story of this country—plenty of talent around but so much of it goes to waste. In America a kid like Angie'd have a scholarship, personal trainer, counsellor, lots of help to get through the rough spots. Here, it's just sink or swim.'

'Have you got any idea where she got the steroids from?'

He shook his head. 'Naw, could be anywhere. They're fuckin' available.'

'Is it a big business? I mean, money involved?'

'You bet it is. How many of those footballers use 'em d'you reckon? I'll tell you, a hell of a lot. And this stuff that's going on now won't stop it. Plus the runners, rowers, gymnasts, weight-lifters, hockey . . . '

'I thought there were tests?'

'There's ways to dodge the tests. There's a quid in all that as well.'

'But you don't know of a source?'

'I wouldn't piss on anyone connected with it if they were on fire. Clinton asked me the same question and I gave him the same answer. Tell you what, I wouldn't like to be in the shoes of whoever gave Angie the stuff when Clinton catches up with him.'

'You say *when* he catches him?'

'Clinton said he'd destroy whoever was responsible and I believe him. That boy was ripped apart.'

'So why isn't he around looking, asking questions, helping the police?'

Carey shrugged. 'Search me. Maybe he is. Maybe he had to go interstate or to New Zealand. Some of the stuff comes from over there. I'll tell you one thing though, he was fair dinkum.'

'I'm told he was drinking a bit after Angela went into hospital.'

'Wouldn't you? Yeah, the time I had this talk with him he'd had a few, but he wasn't cracking up. He was white-hot angry. I could've used that anger on the court and I was sorry I couldn't tap into it. Bloody sorry. My job depends on results.'

'He wasn't suicidal?'

He looked at me as if I'd asked him to spell cat. 'Clint? Never! Murderous more like. You'll have to excuse me, I've got to try and turn a couple of these lunks into point scorers.'

He jogged off and I left the court after a quick glance at the hoop. It still seemed a long way up. I waved to Kathy and walked out into sunshine that made me hot in my leather jacket. I stripped it off and breathed in the rain-cleared air. The running track was away to the left and I could see figures in bright singlets circling it at a steady pace. I wondered what it was like to go to university on a sports scholarship. A lot of fun, probably, but there was no such thing in my day, and they still wouldn't offer them for surfing and boxing.

I began to walk towards my car and a young man jumped in front of me with an upraised hand like a traffic cop, 'Mr Hardy?'

I didn't like being stopped like that so I kept walking, forcing him to step aside and trot beside me. That was better.

'Mr Hardy?'

'That's right. Who might you be?'

'I'm Mark Alessio. I'm the editor of the student paper here. Also the chief reporter and sports reporter.

I slowed down. 'And who put you on to me, Mr Alessio?'

'I can't say. Could you stop for a minute. I'd like to talk to you.'

I slowed down. 'Friend of Kathy's, are you?'

He smiled. 'Ah, a journalist can't reveal his sources.'

I laughed and stopped. He was around twenty, tallish with long blond hair. Definitely Kathy's type. He wore jeans, sneakers, a windcheater and a sleeveless denim jacket. The motorcycle helmet and backpack he carried had slowed him down. He reached into the backpack and took out a notebook.

'What's that for?' I said.

'I want to interview you.'

'Want's one thing, doing it's another. I don't think I have anything to say to the student press just now, Mr Alessio.'

'I'm researching what happened to Angela Cousins.'

That was a pretty good line. He got my attention. I slung my jacket over my shoulder and looked him in the eye. 'And I'm looking into the disappearance of Clinton Scott, although that statement's not on the record so don't write it down.'

He clicked his ballpoint instead of writing. 'I know you are. D'you think the two things are connected?'

'Good try.'

'I want to help.'

'To do what?'

'Find out who supplied Angie with the steroids.'

'That's not supposed to be public knowledge.'

'It isn't, but I can find things out.'

He said it without boastfulness and I gave him points for that. 'Did you know Angie well?'

'Not as well as I wanted to, but any hopes I might have had went out the window when the Black Prince came along.'

'You don't like him?'

'He was bad news for women. I could name you three or four he dumped—what's the word?—unceremoniously. And now he's gone. No, I don't like him. Maybe *he* gave Angie the drugs.'

'Is that your theory?'

'I don't know. I'm considering it while I scratch around.'

'Doing what?'

'Talking to the jocks, hanging out around the gyms, picking up gossip. Maybe that's what you should be doing. I thought perhaps we could pool our resources.'

'My job's to find Clinton Scott. Nothing more than that.'

'Well, good luck and thanks for nothing. One thing's for sure, you won't find him around here today.'

'Oh, why's that?'

He sneered at me. He didn't sneer very well. It's hard to do. All it did was make him look very upset and very, very young. 'Hadn't you heard? They're switching Angie off today.'

6

There was no way I was going to front up to Mrs Cousins now. The contradictory assessments I'd been given of Clinton Scott's character didn't bother me too much—people are complex and present different facets to different parties—but they certainly didn't help me to get a line on what might have happened to him. There was some kind of agreement that he was out to get those responsible for what had happened to Angela, but also a scepticism about whether he was sincere or capable. There'd been no passport in the house at Helensburgh. I'd have to check with Wesley as to whether he had one. If so, Carey's suggestion about New Zealand might have some merit. If he'd gone interstate why not take his car? Unless he intended to leave no tracks.

I'd have to find out about his bank accounts and credit cards—routine stuff that I'd jumped over in the hope of hitting on something solid right off. Bad procedure. At least there was no bad news to confront Wesley with—no signs that he was suicidal or that he'd come to harm. He'd been emotionally shattered, that was clear. It wasn't unusual for a Don Juan to fall hard when he fell. His behaviour had altered, as evidenced by the drinking and he'd vanished, apparently of his own accord. It wasn't comforting for the Scott family but it could have been worse.

Since serving a gaol sentence for tampering with evidence and other offences and since the retirement of Frank Parker, my stocks with the New South Wales police department have fallen. I used to be able to invoke Frank's name to get at least grudging cooperation at fairly senior levels. Not any more. The clean-up of the force has worked to a degree which means that the corrupt are more covert, the honest are more careful, and everyone is more secretive.

I drove to the Campbelltown police station where I was treated politely by some young uniformed men and women but made to kick my heels for an hour waiting until Detective Sergeant Morton Grace could find the time to see me. I reflected that in my day cops had names like Frank Parker and Col Williamson. As I sat in the station I tried to work out what was different about the atmosphere. The decor was drab, the noticeboard was untidy and the floor was scuffed and in need of a mop. Then it came to me—the air smelled of sweat, dust and damp but not of tobacco smoke. The old-time cops worked in a fug that would have put this new breed in an oxygen tent.

Eventually Grace came down the stairs and beckoned to me. He was blocky in build with a thick, dark moustache and cropped hair. Neither his shirt nor his tie nor his suit pants looked expensive—that's something the plain clothes men avoid these days. We shook' hands and I followed him upstairs to his office. It was a cubbyhole off a big room where several detectives sat about using telephones and computers. Again, no smoke. There was just room in the office for a desk, two chairs and a filing cabinet. Grace waved to a chair, sat down himself and looked at his watch.

'I can give you fifteen minutes, Hardy,' he said. 'If you need that long.'

I'd rehearsed what I'd say while I was waiting and I gave him the spiel, emphasising the possibility of a connection between the disappearance of Clinton Scott and Angela Cousins' misadventure. Grace had some papers on his desk which he referred to as I spoke. When I finished he looked up.

'That occurred to me when I was looking this stuff over,' he said. 'But there's not much to go on, is there? No sign of Scott and of course we couldn't even talk to the girl, poor kid. No-one had any idea where she got the stuff.'

'Did any of your people talk to Clinton Scott at the time?'

'No.'

'Why not? They were an item.'

'No-one told us. Fact is, we didn't get a whole lot of cooperation. The parents were too upset and the sporting fraternity closed ranks. The mere mention of steroids scares the shit out of them.'

'And you've got no clues on the source?'

He shook his head. 'It's a very private business. Not like dealing dope or smack. It could've been any one of a number of sports trainers, or a doctor or a vet.'

'A vet?'

He flicked through the papers. 'The chemical analysis suggests that some of the stuff she used was intended for animals.'

'Jesus. Did you know that they're turning off the life support today?'

He clicked his tongue. 'That'd make it a very serious charge if anything could be proved. Any chance that Scott was involved?'

'None, I'd say.'

'But you would say that, wouldn't you?' He looked at his watch again and shifted in his seat. 'I'm busy, sorry. Look, a description of Scott's been circulated and the usual processes put in place. You know what they're worth. I'm sorry about the girl. It'll depend on what the Coroner says as to what further action goes on there, but again, I wouldn't hold my breath for a result.'

I thought I'd save myself one piece of work anyway so I asked if Clinton Scott held a passport. Grace said he didn't know, and that, along with the feeble attempt to interview Noel Kidman, gave me an idea of how thorough the investigation had been and what justification Wesley had for his scepticism. I thanked Grace for his time and left.

My car was a block away. I walked it without taking any notice of my surroundings or the people in the street. It looked as if I'd come to a dead end and had nothing to offer my client. Not a comfortable feeling. I tried to tell myself that the people I'd use to track Clinton's paper and plastic trail would come up with something, but I didn't convince myself.

Mark Alessio was sitting sideways on his motor-cycle parked behind my car. He held a mobile phone in his hand and tears were rolling down his cheeks.

He looked up and saw me. 'She's gone,' he said.

I echoed Morton Grace. 'I'm sorry.'

He closed up the phone and shoved it into the pocket of his jacket. 'Sure.'

'Would you mind telling me what you're doing here?'

'I followed you. I wanted to see if you were serious about this. Did you talk to the police about Angie?'

I felt intensely sorry for him. To lose someone you care deeply about at that age is hard. I'd seen that sort of experience twist and distort young people, make them violent or reduce them to ciphers. It all depended on the strength of the character under stress. Mark Alessio seemed to be resourceful, a big point in his favour in my book. I told him I had talked about Angela Cousins and also that the officer had suggested, as he had done, that Clinton Scott had been the culprit.

Alessio shook his head. 'That was just malice. I don't really think so. I don't know what to think.'

'Neither do I. Did Angie have any close friends, women say, who might have some idea of where she was headed?'

'I don't think so. She worked very hard at her courses, so her teachers tell me. She was a journalism major. I tried to get her to write for the paper but she wouldn't. She trained like a demon, Tanya Martyn says. Work and training, that was it, until the Prince came along. But, like I say, he wasn't a sports sleaze.'

'Who gave him that nickname—the Black Prince?'

Alessio almost grinned, the first non-grim expression I'd seen on him. 'I did, in the paper. Inspired by jealousy, but accurate enough. I'm totally unco, can't throw a Coke can into a rubbish bin at three paces, especially if there's someone watching me. But I'm not quitting the way fucking Clinton did. I'm going to follow this through.'

'Good on you,' I took a card from my wallet and gave it to him. 'Give me a call if you think I can help.' I dug into the wallet again and took out a fifty dollar note. He swayed back and held up his hands. I put the note on the petrol tank of his bike. 'Buy a wreath for Angie,' I said.

7

And that was it. I put the computer jockeys onto tracing Clinton's bank accounts and learned nothing useful. There'd been one big withdrawal since he went missing and nothing since. Wesley told me that Clinton didn't have a passport, so that was a dead end as well. I talked to Noel Kidman again and learned nothing new. He was grateful for the breathing space Wesley was giving him and thought it might just see him through. I wished him luck and told him where to return the car when the semester was over.

I talked to the coach of the football team Clinton played for. Like Leo Carey he was resentful at the absence of one of his best players. He said that Clinton had turned up drunk at training, been disciplined and hadn't shown up again.

'Pity,' he said. 'That kid had potential.'

I tracked down some of Clinton's schoolfriends and university classmates and team-mates. None had seen him or had any idea where he might have gone. I located a former girlfriend, a stunning looking redhead football groupie who'd latched on to Clinton after a game and clung for a while. She wasn't bitter about him. He'd treated her well while they were together but made it clear that it wouldn't last. When I asked if he was likely to get back with her, on the rebound from Angela as it were, she laughed.

'There'd be three or four in line ahead of me,' she said.

A newspaper clipping arrived in the mail. It was from the student paper, the *Southwestern Star*, and gave an account of the career and death of Angela Cousins along with a photograph. It didn't state that her death was due to the use of steroids; there was a reference to 'aberrant reactions to medication', but you could read between the lines. Even the cheap production couldn't dim the beauty and optimism in the young woman's face. I assumed Mark Alessio had sent it but there was no accompanying note. I put the clipping in the file I'd opened with my meagre notes and a short newspaper article on the Coroner's finding of death by misadventure.

I exhausted all the avenues I could think of and reported my failure to Wesley. I submitted a list of the people I'd talked to along with my expenses. He surveyed the document gloomily.

'I can see you've put in the time, Cliff. That's terrible about the girl. I wish we'd known about her, but I guess Clinton was still too angry about what his sister said. I think Mandy backed her up as well. Shit.'

'He took it hard it seems. Well, you said he's like that. The thing is, if someone intelligent and resourceful really wants to hide, he or she can. All

I can say is that there's absolutely no indication that he was suicidal or that he ran into trouble. That's not to say that he won't.'

'Explain.'

We were in the gym. I'd done a work-out after missing several sessions and it'd been hard. I was beginning to see that this exercise business was a lifelong commitment and I'd never been good at things like that.

I towelled off and stretched to ease my aching shoulder muscles. 'All the signs are that he set out to expose the people who'd given Angela the steroids. The word that came up was destroy. That's a tough word. I know bugger-all about it, but I'm told there's big money in performance-enhancing substances.'

Wesley snorted. 'Tell me about it. I saw it all when I was into body-building. But they're sleazes, those guys. Losers.'

'Maybe then,' I said. 'Not now, I suspect. Some of these athletes are earning really big bucks and their contracts require them to keep on performing. It's a forcing house for drug abuse. If Clinton goes in boots and all against that sort of money he's headed for trouble. The people behind it are organised, you can bet, and have muscle protection.'

'And you've got no idea of where he might've looked.'

'None. Do you?'

Wesley shook his head. 'In London, in the old days, sure. But not here. I could ask around but that'd be difficult in my line of work. You know what I mean. We have to be squeaky clean.'

'I don't,' I said. 'I'll ask around.'

Wes wrote me a cheque. Before he handed it to me he said, 'What if I hired you to look into this steroid business? If you found out where that girl had got the stuff we could deal with it and maybe Clinton ... '

'You're grasping at straws, Wes. I could spend months on it and come up with nothing. I know you're making a quid here, but you wouldn't want to be shelling out a grand a week.'

'You mean you don't want to do it?'

'I'm just saying, let's not formalise it. I'll ask around, but I mean it'd be unprofessional to make a contract. It's outside my field of competence.'

'Clinton's got no competence at all as an investigator of any bloody thing. The way you tell it the next I'm likely to hear of him is that he's dead in a ditch.'

'Do you remember how it felt—the first girl you were crazy about?'

'Yeah, madness.'

'The chances are that's the story here. A lot worse of course, given what's happened. But you get over it. He'll turn up. As I say, I'll keep an ear out.'

I took the cheque and I continued to do my work-outs and have my massages. But the atmosphere had changed. Wesley was morose and I felt that he thought I'd given up on his son. I didn't feel that I had, but I didn't feel good about it either. I made some enquiries about likely steroid pushers and came up with nothing. After four or five weeks I stopped going to the gym.

Three months later I finished a remunerative and happily uneventful bodyguarding job. I was contemplating a short springtime holiday on the central coast on the strength of a respectable bank balance for once. I was tossing up about locations and wondering if I might be able to persuade Terry Kenneally to come with me. It depended on whether she could take a break from tennis coaching and how she'd feel about an indecent invitation from someone she hadn't heard from in six months. I rated my chances as only fair or worse. I consulted the touring map and I'd decided on Nambucca Heads and was about to call Terry when the phone rang.

'Hardy? This is Morton Grace from Campbell-town.'

Morton Grace—an impossible name to forget. 'Yes, Sergeant.'

'D'you remember a kid named Mark Alessio, student at the university here?'

'Yes.'

'Had any contact with him since?'

I said I hadn't, then I remembered the anonymous newspaper clipping, but I let the answer stand. 'Why?'

'He was killed in a hit and run the day before yesterday. A witness says it looked deliberate. Station wagon. We found your card in his wallet. I thought you might know what he'd been up to.'

I remembered giving him the card and the

money, remembered his distress and determination. I felt the weight of it—two bright, promising young people dead and one missing.

'Hardy, you there?'

'Yes. He fancied himself as an investigative reporter. He was interested in the death of a student athlete. Maybe he found something out. Have you got any leads other than the station wagon?'

'Thanks, Hardy.' He rang off. I put the phone down and folded up the map.

Call it what you like, guilt, conscience or simply reluctance to leave a job undone, but I figured I'd feel better if I put in some more work on the Clinton Scott disappearance. It was of long standing by this time and now I had a starting point. I rang the university, got through to the sports centre and asked to speak to Kathy Simpson.

A man answered the phone. 'She's not on right now.'

In the old days you could ask institutions for people's phone numbers and addresses and get them, not any more.

'I see. When will she be on?'

'Let me check. Ah, she took a two-day sickie. Should be on again this evening.'

I thanked him and rang off. I was grasping at straws the way Wesley had wanted me to. I was sure that Kathy had steered Mark Alessio to me. He'd smirked slightly when I named her and he'd responded by saying he couldn't reveal his sources. Kathy's taking two days off tended to confirm the connection. It was a bit stronger than a straw, a stick maybe.

I spent the afternoon in the new Glebe branch of the Leichhardt library fumbling my way around on the Internet looking for information on steroids. I discovered that all anabolic steroids, although they travelled under a variety of names, were essentially synthetic versions of the male hormone testosterone. The material was abundant and somewhat contradictory. Some sources insisted that moderate use of steroids was completely safe and enhanced recovery from injury, muscle building, aerobic fitness and that the increased muscle mass boosted confidence and the competitive spirit. The pro-steroid people said that negative reactions—baldness and testicle atrophy in men, hairiness and interference in menstrual cycles in women—were completely reversible when the steriod-taking stopped or was reduced. I waded through the psycho-medical jargon in a long article which concluded that studies of the effects of steroids on human moods were inconclusive.

The anti-steroid brigade was strident and vociferous. One article simply listed scores of adverse side-effects that had been detected in athletes using steroids and regarded that as Q.E.D. Another writer said that the supposed beneficial effects were illusory or temporary at best. It was claimed that some of the side-effects, particularly the masculinisation of women, were irreversible. The moral aspect came into play for some analysts who insisted, with athletes like Carl Lewis, that steroid-users were nothing more than cheats and should be treated accordingly. 'They should be treated the way a golfer at the Augusta Masters who threw his ball out of a bunker would be—banned!'

What both camps agreed on was the danger involved in using black-market steroids produced under questionable conditions and likely to be adulterated. A sober medical study detailed the ways steroid use could kill you. The liver and the heart were viewed as particularly vulnerable. Damage to the liver could run from jaundice to a kind of hepatitis and the formation of tumours, both non-cancerous and malignant. Steroid use could cause the heart muscles to grow rapidly, leaving an area of tissue which was inadequately supplied with blood because the blood vessels couldn't cope. Heart cells could die and a fatal heart attack could result. I wondered which of these very unpleasant side-effects had killed Angela Cousins.

I arrived at the sports centre at 5.30. Kathy was behind the desk but not looking her former perky self. Her eyes were red-rimmed and her shoulders drooped. I watched her going about her tasks for a few minutes before I approached. Reluctant wasn't the word. She looked half-dead.

'Hello, Kathy. Remember me?'

She looked at me dully. 'No. Sorry.'

'I'm the private detective who spoke to you about Clinton Scott a few months back. You put me onto Tanya Martyn and then you put Mark Alessio onto me. Remember now?'

The name got a reaction. A spark of interest in her eyes that flared and died. 'Oh, yes. Sure.'

'I was sorry to hear about Mark. You were close to him, weren't you?'

She sniffed. 'I tried to be. Look, I've got things to do . . . '

'I need to talk to you, Kathy. About Mark. It's important. I talked to him a couple of times and he sent me something in the mail. Do you get a break here?'

The idea of talking about Mark seemed to do her some good, as I hoped it would. She nodded. 'In half an hour.'

'We'll have a cup of coffee and a talk.'

She nodded again and took a phone call. A section of the reception area was partitioned off and contained a couple of tables with chairs and a bank of self-serve machines. I sat and waited while Kathy worked. She did her best to be cheerful but it was a struggle. I stopped watching and doodled in my notebook instead. As the trainers and competitors came and went I speculated about which ones could be on steroids. Impossible to tell. I'd read that there were creams and oral treatments now to combat the pimples steroids often caused and more effective depilation procedures for women. There was always the giveaway of the so-called 'roid rages'—uncontrollable, unprovoked, violent outbursts that had caused steroid users to injure themselves and others. But all was calm in the Southwestern University sports centre.

Tanya Martyn strode in and stopped when she

saw me. She was wearing medium heels, a short, tight grey skirt and a red blazer. She was carrying a sports bag that looked heavy. I got up and went towards her.

'Hello.' She dropped the bag and clicked her fingers.

'Hardy,' I said. 'Cliff Hardy.'

'Oh, yes.'

Suddenly, I was tongue-tied. I was attracted to her but I was out of practice at talking to attractive woman. I almost said something inane like, 'I bet you're glad it's not raining.' Instead I muttered something about how her team was going and she replied non-committedly. We exchanged smiles and that was it. She went up a flight of stairs with her back straight and the muscles in her legs moving smoothly. I judged that she'd forgotten me as soon as she reached the top. She was, as the commentators say these days, *focused*.

Kathy came over and slumped into a chair.

'Coffee?'

'Please,' she said. 'White with three sugars.'

I fed the coins in and got the polystyrene cups filled. I put the three sachets of sugar and wooden stirrer down beside Kathy's cup. I took mine black, mindful of my slight weight increase since quitting the gym. She drew out the fiddling with the sugar and stirred for as long as she could before she looked up at me.

'I really liked him. He was so clever and so nice, so funny. Me, I'm just a dumb jockette. That's what they call us sporting girls. I'm slowly getting together enough units for a diploma in human movement. A couple to go, but studying's not my scene.'

'The first night I saw you here you were efficient, on top of everything and very helpful to both me and Mark. You shouldn't put yourself down, Kathy. You'll get over this.'

She drank some coffee and sniffed loudly. 'You think so?'

'I know.'

'It's difficult, you see. A lot of women in the sport scene are dykes. They tell you what bastards men are, how weak and unreliable they are. And, you know, you find that's true sometimes. I knew Mark was just on the rebound from Angela Cousins who he'd hardly even spoken to. I mean, that's silly, isn't it? To be in love with a star sportswoman like that when you can hardly . . . '

'Throw a Coke can into a rubbish bin?'

She smiled. 'He told you that?'

I drank some of the bitter, thin coffee and wished I'd put some sugar in it. 'Yeah. And you're right, it is silly. But it happens. So you spent some time with him recently?'

'Uh huh. A bit. We went to the movies a couple of times and to the pub. I helped him with layout and such on the paper. I'm okay at that. We . . . did it three times, no four. I liked it, but . . . but I'm not sure that he did. Oh, shit . . . '

She was drooping again and I had to catch her before she slid down into the misery of indifference where one thing is much the same as another and memories are fuzzy. I leaned forward. 'Kathy, what I need to know is about his investigation into the steroid suppliers. Did he talk to you about that?'

Another sniff. 'Yes, he did. He didn't mention any names because he said it wasn't safe for me to know.'

Great, I thought. *Very honourable. Thank you, Mark.* 'What *did* he say about it?'

She shrugged and drained her cup. 'He said it was all going on in Sydney and out here. And that there was a lot of money in it. He said some athletes took out loans to buy the steroids because they thought taking them'd get them prize money and sponsors and that.'

'He didn't say where the buying and selling happened?'

'No. But I'll tell you one thing he said that'll interest you, Mr Hardy. I've just remembered. I've got a lousy memory. Mark said he'd met someone who'd seen and talked to Clinton Scott.'

8

She was fragile and needed careful handling. 'When was this?' I said quietly.

'Mark said it must've been not long after Angela went into hospital.'

'I see. And where did this happen?'

'In Bingara. Mark went down there after she died, to talk to her family. He said one of them told him this young West Indian guy had been hanging around a few weeks before.'

'What did Mark think about that?'

She shrugged and glanced at the clock. Her break time was running out. 'He didn't say much about it. Didn't even say who'd told him. Mark didn't like Clinton for obvious reasons. Look, I have to get back.'

'Okay, thanks Kathy. You've been a big help. I might need to talk to you again. Would that be all right?'

'Sure. What're you going to do now?'

'Go to Bingara.'

'Yeah. All these blokes chasing after Angela Cousins, even when she's dead. I guess that's star quality.'

'I'm still after Clinton, but it begins to look as if that could have something to do with what happened to Mark. It's a possibility anyway. Doesn't that matter to you?'

'No. Why should it? He's gone. That's all that matters to me. I'm not interested in revenge or any of that male shit. Thanks for the coffee. Excuse me.'

She went back to work and threw herself into it, checking schedules, making up program cards, making phone calls. She carefully avoided looking my way. I got another cup of coffee and added whitener and sugar. I stirred the sugar in and pondered my next move. It sounded as if the sighting of Clinton Scott postdated his disappearance from Helensburgh and Campbelltown. To that extent it was encouraging and certainly worth following up. Not encouraging enough though to make contact with Wesley. I'd have to put in some more work on my own time and come up with more solid information to justify that.

I headed south on the motorway, bypassing Wollongong and Kiama and picking up the Princes Highway through Nowra. It was early in the week and early in the good weather season so traffic was light. I calculated I could make Ulladulla for the night and get into Bingara the next morning. Nowra had expanded since I'd last been there some years back and I suspected that the story would be same all the way down the coast. Why not? These days, with the cars and roads the way they are, you can live in Sydney and have a weekender at Jervis Bay. I wouldn't mind.

I reached Ulladulla soon after nine and checked into a Flag motel. I like motels and fancy the idea of managing one in the right spot, on the North Coast or in Queensland, say, when I get too old for the game I'm in now. With proper organisation, I reckon that could give me plenty of time for swimming, reading, fishing, drinking wine and observing human nature. For now, this was just another motel night the way I've spent too many, alone. I bought a hamburger in a cafe across the road and ate it with a can of light beer from the minibar. I watched a documentary on TV about the connection between heart transplants and retirement. That kind of took the gloss off the Queensland motel idea.

I made Bingara by mid-morning on a day that started out mild but was going to warm up fast. In the bad old days when you wanted to find the Aborigines in a country town, you located the camp on the river or creek or, in the worst cases, out by the town rubbish dump. Things have changed for the better and the Aborigines live in the towns and not always clustered together. I drove around the place for a few minutes, just enjoying the view out over the estuary to the sea and the way the town settled in between some low hills and the sand dunes.

The local phone book in the post office-cum-general store gave me the number of the Bingara Aboriginal Progressive Association. I rang it on my mobile and a woman answered in the distinctive tones of Aboriginal speech. I identified myself and said I was trying to get in touch with the Roberts family.

'Are you a Koori, Mr Hardy?'

'No, I'm not.'

'Can you tell me the reason for your enquiry?'

'I'm looking for a young man named Clinton Scott. He was close to Angela Cousins who died recently. I believe he came down here to make contact with Angela's mother's family. That's Mrs Julie Cousins whose maiden name was Roberts. I was told by someone else who came down to talk to the Roberts family that a family member met Clinton Scott here. That's the last reported sighting of this young man and I want to follow it up.'

'Have you spoken to Mrs Cousins?'

'No, but I met Mr Cousins a couple of months ago. He told me about his wife's connection with Bingara. If you were to ring him in Parramatta I think he'd vouch for me.'

'Hold on, please.'

I sat in the car with the windows down, hoping to catch some breeze. I was wearing a short-sleeved shirt and linen trousers, but a T-shirt and shorts would have been more appropriate. I wondered who she was talking to and about what and was getting impatient when she came back on the line.

'This someone else you're referring to, would that be Mark Alessio?'

'Yes.'

'I believe he had a conversation with Daniel Roberts in the Fisherman's Rest hotel.'

That's how it is in these small places. You can't scratch yourself without someone noticing and passing the information on to somebody else. 'Thank you. Where would I find Mr Roberts?'

'You'll find him in the Fisherman's Rest hotel.' Her voice was full of regret and disapproval.

I thanked her and rang off. Bingara town centre essentially consisted of a street running north–south crossed by two running east–west. I got out of the car, looked east and saw the hotel on the corner a block away. It was 11 a.m. on a hot day and the Fisherman's Rest hotel didn't sound like a bad port of call. I drove the block, parked in a skerrick of shade, and crossed the street to the pub. Its design was classical—two-storeyed with a wide balcony on the top level supported by skinny uprights. On a busy hot night the drinkers would spill out onto the tiled area under the balcony, lean on the posts and shoot the shit. But there was no-one out there now. The drinkers were all inside, sensibly sheltering from the midday sun.

I went in, took off my sunglasses and let my eyes adjust to the light. There's something harmonious about an Australian country pub if the licensee gets it right. The parts all fit together— the tin and wood on the bar, the mottled mirror behind the spirits bottles, the blackboard with the counter lunch menu chalked up. There were four men in the bar lined up on stools with beers in front of them. Two were Aborigines, two were white men. The barmaid was middle-aged, fat, blonde and looked ready to cope with anything that came at her from the other side of the bar. She had an unlit cigarette in her mouth that jiggled when she spoke.

'Morning. What can I do you for?'

One of the drinkers snorted his amusement at a greeting he must have heard a thousand times before.

'Middy of Reschs, thanks. No, make it a schooner. She's warm outside.'

She drew the beer expertly. 'You're a bit early for the holiday season. Mind you, we can get some lovely weather this time of year.'

I sipped the beer, the best drink on earth on a hot day and not so bad on a cold one. 'I believe you. It's a great spot. But I'm working.'

It suited me to bait her a little. In places like this the ice needed breaking and it was better that you answered questions rather than volunteer information. I was betting that the barmaid had had all the conversations she'd ever need to have with the four men present. I shot them a quick look as I worked on the schooner. They wore the air of absolutely comfortable regulars whose every word and gesture would be familiar and hold no surprises. The barmaid was a talker and needed stimulation. She reached under the counter, found two saucers, gave them a wipe with her cloth and took a couple of packets of beer nuts from the rack near the cigarettes. The drinkers watched her with interest. This was evidently something unusual. She spilled nuts into the saucers, placed the fullest one for the four locals to share and put the other in front of me.

'Help yourself.'

'Thanks.' I took a few nuts and chewed them. They were stale but I didn't let on.

'You going to want lunch? We've got good fish, steak if you prefer.'

'Yes, maybe.' A noisy truck went by outside and I dropped my voice. 'Would one of these blokes be Daniel Roberts?'

She looked at me closely, taking in the broken nose and other signs. 'I should've known. Bloody boxing. Danny! Bloke here wants to talk to you.'

My face might bear the marks of a few fists and beatings with other objects, but the face that turned towards us was one sculptured by pugilism. His nose was a flattened ruin, the heavy eyebrow ridges were a mass of scar tissue and his mouth and ears had been pulped into shapelessness. He stood. I was expecting a drunken lurch but he advanced steadily and stuck out his hand. He was sober or very nearly so.

'Gidday,' he said. 'I'm Danny Roberts. Journalist are you, mate?'

The name clicked then. Danny Roberts had been a journeyman welterweight in those years Joe Cousins had described as the doldrums. The fighters made lousy money, endured bad managers, mismatches and crooked promoters and were lucky to come out of it with their health. Whether Roberts had or not I couldn't be sure. His speech was clear and he didn't have any of the tics that afflict brain-damaged fighters.

I stuck out my hand and we shook. 'No,' I said. 'Not a journalist. I'm a private detective.'

'Yeah? Never met one of them before. I've met a few of the public ones.'

I grinned with him and felt at ease. I began to tell him what I was about but he stopped me and suggested that we go over to a table where we could talk in private.

'Buy you a drink?' I said.

'Sure. Middy of light.'

I'd made a fair impact on the schooner. I tossed it down, got two middies of light and joined Roberts at a table. 'Have to be careful talking Koori business in public,' he said. 'That bloke at the bar'd be all ears and probably get it wrong when he blabbed to the nutters.'

'Nutters?'

'There's people around here, blackfellers, who reckon we should kick all the whitefellers out and take the country back.'

'Big ask.'

'Fuckin' right. Madness. And most of 'em'd be stuffed when the beer ran out. Me, I'm a moderate. Get everything we can, every bloody thing, and don't worry about what we can't get.'

'Sounds right to me. Mind you, I can understand the other point of view.'

'Me, too. But this isn't fuckin' South Africa. Now, what Kooris have you talked to about this?'

'Only Joe Cousins and the woman on the phone at the Aboriginal Progressive Association.'

'Beatrix,' he said. 'Good lady, but a dead-set wowser. Because I come in here for a couple of beers in the middle of the day she reckons I'm a lost cause. Okay, she steered you to me and she's right. I talked to your bloke. Young feller, like you say, West Indian, but he said his name was George.'

I fished out the photo of Clinton and showed it to him.

'Yeah, that's him. Hair was longer but that's him all right. Good looking kid, good build on him. Tall middleweight. Cruiser, maybe.'

'What did he want to talk about?'

'Ah . . . hold on, d'you want something to eat?'

I did. We went across to the counter and ordered steaks with chips and salad. I told Danny Roberts I could put the cost of the meal on my expenses and he shrugged his acceptance. When we sat down with our ticket I noticed that the other Aborigine had left the bar. A few drinkers and lunchers, white and black, had wandered in but we still had our privacy at the table.

'All he wanted to talk about was Angie and the Cousinses. Now Angie, she's my . . . fuck it, second cousin or something. We just call it family, you know? Julie, her mum, used to bring her down here for holidays when she was little. Beautiful little girl. She could run like a greyhound. And jump? You never seen anything like it. She jumped over this creek out in the bush once. I wasn't there but the others told me about it and I went out and measured it. It was seventeen fuckin' feet. Now that's a hell of a jump for a thirteen-year-old in bare feet off grass onto grass.'

I drank some beer and nodded. 'Did you know about what had happened to Angie when

Clinton . . . George, was talking to you?'

Roberts shook his head. 'Knew she was in hospital and pretty crook, but I didn't know she was in a coma and that. The women would've known. Sometimes they keep things like that secret from the men.'

'What else?'

The kitchen hand shouted our number and we went across and collected our plates. The steaks were big and well done. The chips were crisp and the salad contained slices of tinned beetroot and that was fine by me. We both ate a few mouthfuls and drank some beer.

'All right?'

'Bloody good.'

'Mine's all the fuckin' better for being paid for by you. Okay, now George wanted me to tell him things about the Koori way.'

'What things?'

He masticated a mouthful of steak, plucked out a sliver of bone and grinned at me. 'I couldn't tell him and I can't tell you. He might've had a brown skin but he was just as much a whitefeller as you as far as I was concerned. I showed him some blackfeller fishing tricks. No harm in that. Oh, and we had a day out in the bush and I learned him a bit about hunting and that, bush-tucker stuff. But he wanted to know how I felt about the country and what things mean to me. Couldn't tell him much. Hard, because he was real sincere about it.'

'How'd he take it?'

'Bad. Very upset, like it was the end of the world. Got pissed. I have to tell you he was a

76

terrible drinker. I mean, he fuckin' *tried* to drink and he did. But it didn't take much to get him rotten.'

'How many times did you see him?'

'A few times.' He jabbed his fork at the table. 'Mostly in here.'

'And when was this, exactly?'

'Mate, exactly is a bit hard for me. I'm on a pension, see. Do a bit of fishing and odd jobs, but one day's much the same as the next and the weeks sort of run on. It was a fair while ago. That's about all I can tell you.'

We kept eating, exchanged a few remarks about the food, finished our drinks and he got up to get another round. We were Cliff and Danny by now and I asked him if he'd liked Clinton.

'Yeah, well enough. Nice young bloke when he wasn't pissed. He got me to teach him a few things about boxing. Wish I hadn't.'

'Why's that?'

'He got into a fight one night when he was drunk. Right here it was. Picked on a big black-feller and got the shit beat out of him. He was knocked about real bad and on top of that *he* was the one got thrown in the lockup. I reckon the copper thought he was just another Abo.'

'What happened to him after that?'

'I dunno, mate. Like I told that young feller from the university, I never saw him again. Reckon you'd have to ask the copper.'

9

I was tossing up whether to pay Danny Roberts for the information he'd given me when he finished his last mouthful of food, downed his beer, wiped his mouth, put his knife and fork together and stood up.

'Gotta catch the tide, Cliff. Should be a few sand whiting about.'

'Good luck, Danny. And thanks. By the way, what's the policeman's name?'

We shook hands.

'Pipe,' he said. 'Sergeant Pipe. Goes by the nickname of Copper, but not to his face, mind.'

'Right.'

'I hope you find the kid and that he's not in too much trouble. But from the fuckin' look of him I'd say that's where he was headed. I know the signs. Thanks for the tucker. See you.'

He gave a wave to the fat barmaid as he walked out. I cleaned up my plate and put down the rest of the beer, thinking that to live on a pension in a place like this and do some fishing and odd jobs couldn't be too bad. Then I remembered that he'd said he lived on his own and I knew the downside of that. He'd befriended a young man who'd got into trouble and left without saying goodbye. He had a lot of dignity and resilience: all things considered, Danny Roberts was one of life's lucky people.

A passer-by directed me to the police station, a newish brick building with a well-maintained lawn around it and neatly trimmed hedges. I wondered if the temporary occupants of the lockup cut the grass and the privet. Probably. I went through a screen door that had ENTER painted on it. The interior was air-conditioned and smelled of floor polish and scented cleaner. Sergeant Pipe had some good backup. There was a high counter closing the working space off from the citizenry. A big man in the uniform of the NSW police force was sitting behind a desk reading a facsimile sheet.

I cleared my throat. 'Sergeant Pipe?'

He looked up. 'Be with you in a minute, mate.'

He finished reading the sheet, made a note in the margin and put it aside. He took off his reading glasses and tucked them away in his shirt pocket. He got to his feet, not without effort. He was built big and overweight with it so that he had a lot to move. He shifted the pistol on his hip as he advanced to the counter but I was sure that was just for his own comfort. I'd taken my sunglasses off and couldn't look threatening in my short-sleeved shirt and linen pants. I smelled of beer and onions, but he must've been used to that.

I opened up the folder with my PEA licence and laid it on the desk for him to inspect. He looked at it as if he wanted to put it through a shredder. He was about fifty and going to seed fast. Not open to new experiences, I judged, not a lover of humanity.

'Yes?' he growled.

'I'm working on a missing person case,' I said. I took out Clinton's picture and held it up for him. 'I understand this young man was here some time back and that you arrested him?'

His eyes flicked over the photograph but gave nothing away. 'Who told you that?'

'Danny Roberts.'

'Should mind his own bloody business, but, yeah, I had him in for a night. So what?'

I produced the copy of the report Wesley had filed with the police at Helensburgh. The official document seemed to molify him somewhat. He took the glasses out and scanned it. 'Says here this bloke's name's Clinton Scott.'

'Same man though. What name did you book him under, sergeant?'

'Don't remember.' He reached under the counter and pulled up a heavy ledger book. 'All in here. Have to put it on bloody computers nowadays. I get the wife to do that of a Sunday night, but I go by this.'

He wet his finger and turned over the leaves. 'Here he is. Drunk and disorderly, 10 June. George Cousins.'

The date placed Clinton in Bingara shortly after the verdict was pronounced on Angela and was the only firm record of his existence after his disappearance from Helensburgh and the university.

I made a note and tried to read the entry but the writing was faint and illegible.

'What happened? Was he fined or what?'

Sergeant Pipe closed the ledger and for a moment I thought he was going to close off all information but the reverse happened. He removed his glasses and leaned on the counter, almost matey. 'I'll tell you. Just to show you city types that we don't treat the blackfellers too bad around here. In the first place, he was banged up real bad in the fight he had with Ernie Carter. Silly bugger shouldn've never taken Ernie on. Had no chance. Anyway, he had a busted nose, cracked cheekbone, couple of teeth out and some cuts that needed stitches. I took him to the clinic here in town and got him fixed up. No charge.'

So I'd been dead wrong about Copper Pipe. 'That was decent of you.'

'Yeah. He'd lost some blood. I didn't want him dying on me in the lockup, did I? Now normally, he would've gone up before the beak on the Monday, this was a Friday night, after a couple of nights in the lockup.'

And cut some grass and trimmed some hedges, I thought.

'But he told me he had this job lined up on a boat that was leaving on the Saturday morning. Charter boat. One of the hands had got sick and young George had talked himself into the job. So, on the Saturday, I takes him down to the jetty and there she is, bloody great sea-going yacht. And I escort George on board. I explain that he's been the victim of an assault. The owner's all sympathy and he takes George on. Tells him to rest up. I reckon if George played it smart he could rest long enough to learn what he had to do, because he knew bugger-all about boats at that point.'

'How did he get the job, d'you think?'

He sucked his teeth and the action seemed to trigger his need to smoke. He took a packet of cigarettes from his other shirt pocket and offered them to me. I shook my head. He extracted one and moved sideways to open a door that would take him around the counter. When he re-appeared he had the cigarette in his mouth and a lighter in his hand.

'Not allowed to smoke in me own station, would you believe? Time was when the man on the spot made the rules. Not now. Come outside.'

We stood on the concrete porch overlooking the cut grass and the street. Pipe lit up and exhaled luxuriantly. 'Something that feels so bloody good can't be bad for you, that's my philosophy. You're a quiet sort of bloke, Hardy.'

'I'm interested in what you're telling me. I've got a couple more questions and I haven't got an answer to the last one yet.'

'Right, well this boat owner, I forget his name, was about my age and not in much better nick. His wife was a real good-looker and she was younger, a lot younger. I saw the way she looked at George. I reckon he got the job because of her. Just a guess, mind you. But in my game you pick up a bit on those things.'

'I know what you mean.'

'I suppose so. Has George done anything, you

know, dodgy? Struck me as a decent bloke who should stay off the grog.'

There didn't seem to be any point in elaborating. I told Pipe that it was a straight family concern about a missing member.

'Kids,' he said. 'Thank Christ mine're all right. I've got a son in the military and a daughter who's a nurse. You know, you've done me some good, Hardy. That missing person report'll be on the computer. I can respond with a sighting of the subject here. Helps to be able to deal with that sort of stuff.'

'Fine. Now the big questions. What was the name of the boat and where was it heading?'

'*She*, mate, *she*. Boats are female. You're as ignorant as that George was. Well, the name's easy. She was the *Coral Queen*. Beautiful boat.'

'And heading . . . '

'North. That's all I know. North.'

10

I thanked Sergeant Pipe and went in search of Danny Roberts. There were fishermen on the jetty and others strung out at long intervals on the beach. I asked one of the jetty men about Danny and he pointed north.

'He's along there like always. Best part of a mile.'

Walking the best part of a mile, or even the lesser part, in city shoes on soft sand is no fun. About halfway there I was sweating freely and cursing Roberts for not fishing closer to civilisation. When I got close enough to make him out I could see that he was in the act of catching a fish, reeling in, moving back and forward and sideways. I moved nearer and saw him win the battle. He brought the line in with a big flapping fish on the end of it. He unhooked it and tossed it still flapping into a battered Esky.

He was re-baiting the hook when he saw me come up.

'Hey, Cliff. I've caught six. Sell you a couple if you like.'

'No thanks, Danny. Dunno when I'll next be home. Can I have a word?'

'Sure. I'll just toss this in.'

He made his cast with a fluid flick of shoulder, elbow and wrist. The line flew out past the breaking waves. With an action like that he should've done better in the ring. He slotted the butt of the rod into a sleeve embedded in the sand and turned towards me.

'Now . . . ' He gave a whoop as a second rod in the sand bucked. He jumped to it, slid it out and began the same process. I watched, admiring his skill and the obvious intense pleasure he got from what he was doing. If you can make a living doing something you like you've got the game beaten. I sometimes wondered whether it applied to me. He landed the second fish and dealt with it in the same way. When he had both rods re-set he washed his hands in the shallows and indicated that he was ready to talk.

'Sorry about that, mate. Gotta grab 'em while they're there.'

'Right.' I said. 'No problem. Look, Danny, I got the feeling you were a bit pissed off at Clinton . . . George, not saying goodbye.'

'Yeah, a bit.'

'I talked to Copper Pipe. He took him to the clinic and they patched him up. Ah, George told Pipe that he had a job lined up on a boat, starting the next day. He talked Pipe into letting him go away on the boat the next morning instead of going up before the magistrate.'

'That right? Well, he was a good talker.'

'He'd have probably told you about the job if the fight hadn't happened.'

Danny nodded and looked at his rods.

'The thing is, I need to get a line on this boat. It was called the *Coral Queen*. Did you see it?'

'Did I? I'll say. Beautiful craft. Ocean-going yacht. Ketch-rigged with diesel auxiliaries and everything that opened and shut. Be a fuckin' great boat to be on.'

'Did you see the owner?'

'Yeah. Nothin' much of him. A nothin' sort of a bloke, really. Except for the money of course. But no change out of a million for that thing.'

'Did you see his wife?'

Danny winked. 'Who didn't? Marilyn Monroe brought back to life, she was.'

'That good?'

'Yep. She had it and she showed it. Hello!'

The first rod twitched. He took hold of it and did whatever it was he did. This time the contest was over quickly and Danny swore as he reeled in the hook and sinker.

'Fucker threw the hook.'

'Can't catch 'em all.'

'Can try. Why're you asking about the woman?'

'Sergeant Pipe took George to the boat. Kept his eyes open. Like you, he reckoned the owner was a bit past it. He thought the wife had the hots for George and that was how he got the job.'

'Could be, but I doubt it. She'd be wasting her time. Hang on. Think I'll try a worm this time.'

He baited the hook with a length of still-wriggling worm. It was an intricate business and he did it with dexterity and finesse. He made his cast and the action was exactly as before. He sighed with satisfaction as he re-set the rod.

'They say the old people could catch sand-worms with their toes. Buggered if I can. Tried. No way.'

'Why would the wife be wasting her time with George?'

'I heard him make some very nasty remarks about white women.'

'You didn't mention that before.'

Danny nodded. 'It was about the one thing I didn't like about him.'

Clinton Scott was becoming a more complex character with every little bit of information I gained. But at least I was gaining some and had a lead to follow. I wasn't sure, but I assumed that big, expensive boats checked in with some kind of marine authority from time to time. Maybe even notified where they were headed next. A million dollar yacht couldn't be too hard to trace. The new snippet on Clinton was interesting. Hard to interpret though. From what I'd been told, he'd liked white women well enough in the past. I wasn't convinced.

I headed back to Campbelltown, intending to tell Morton Grace about the sighting of Clinton Scott. The further I went the worse the idea seemed. If I told him I'd have to talk about the boat, the wife, Clinton's change of name, maybe even that Danny had told me about his sexual racial preference. I didn't want to say anything about those things to anyone except Wesley and, at this stage, not even to him. I had a course to follow. I was re-plotting myself to Sydney when a truck coming the other way threw up a stone that shattered my windscreen. The glass starred; I punched it out as quickly as I could, cutting my hand, and wrestled with the steering wheel. The Falcon had a tendency to pull to the right and in my momentary loss of control it threatened to swing me off the road and towards some solid gum trees.

A car was coming fast towards me and it sailed past just as I got the Falcon under control and back on the right side of the road. I could feel the adrenaline pumping and the sweat breaking out on my body. I steered the car towards the verge and stopped. I sucked in air and waited for the jitters to pass. I'd known too many people who'd finished up dead on country roads not to feel that I'd had some sort of escape. Again. I was limping towards Ulladulla, peering through the punched hole in the windscreen, pretending that the wind and dust weren't bothering me, when the car started to bump and grind like Tina Turner.

I stopped, got out and was confronted with a flat rear tyre, driver's side. I detached the jack and wheelbrace and changed the wheel in no time at all. When I was young we drove on tyres that were as bald as Yul Brynner and were constantly changing wheels and could do it with our eyes closed. Then we bought thin retreads and did it all over again. I let the car down and it settled lower and lower and lower. The spare clearly had a slow puncture. The motorist's nightmare—two flats.

If I'd limped before I hobbled now into Ulla-dulla. There was a garage opposite the motel I'd stayed in and I put the car in there for a new windscreen and two tyres. I carried my overnight bag across to the motel and booked in again.

'Hullo, Mr Hardy,' the receptionist said brightly. 'Nice to see you again so soon.'

I barely managed a grunt. I went to my room, the same one as before, dropped my bag on the floor and opened the minibar. I poured the miniature bottle of Johnny Walker red over ice and took two decent sips, almost finishing it. I topped the meagre remainder up with water and sat down on the bed. It hadn't been a long day or a hard one, but I felt drained. If I'd kept up the gym work the mile and back along the beach wouldn't have taken so much out of me. I resolved to go back to working out. I finished the drink, kicked off my shoes and went to sleep.

I slept deeply and when I woke up I had the sensation of not knowing where I was or what time of the day or night I was in. The familiar sights and sounds were missing and it took me a few seconds to get my physical bearings and work out the time. The empty glass on the bedside table made sense. My watch told me I'd slept for an hour. It was getting dark outside so that figured. I realised that it was my bladder that had woken me. I stumbled to the bathroom in my socks, had a long piss, climbed out of my clothes and took a hot shower followed by a quick burst of the cold. By the time I'd dried myself, dressed and opened a can of VB, I knew who I was, where I was and what I was supposed to be doing.

I rang through to my number, gave the code and picked up my messages. The first was a miscall, the second was from my personal physician Dr Ian Sangster, proposing a night on the town, and the third was from a young female addicted to the upward inflection.

'Mr Hardy? This is Kathy Simpson? Could you ring me please? I've got something to tell you.'

She gave her number and that was it. Something to tell me? About what? Mark Alessio, what else? I rang the number expecting to get *her* answering machine but got the real live Kathy instead.

'Kathy, this is Cliff Hardy.'

'Oh, hello, Mr Hardy.'

Well, at least it didn't sound like life and death. I told her that I'd got her message and that I was stuck in Ulladulla for the night with car trouble. I asked her what she had to tell me.

'It's more something to show you, really. About Mark's investigation. I was working with him on the paper as I told you and now I've had a look at his files. I couldn't bear to before, but ... '

'I understand. What shift are you on tomorrow?'

'Morning, then I'm at the office of the paper. I could meet you there and show you.'

'That'd be good. I think I can get clear of here by mid-morning. If I'm going to be late I'll ring. What's the number?'

She gave me the number, I wrote it down, thanked her and hung up. My destination was going to be Campbelltown after all.

I thought about calling Wesley Scott but decided the time wasn't right. I wasn't interested in dinner. After the beer I ate the crisps and nuts provided with the complimentary biscuits and called that dinner. To make up for it I ordered a big breakfast. That left some time to kill. Time can fly by in a motel when you're with someone but it crawls when you're on your own. Solitary big breakfasts aren't much fun either.

I've never known instant coffee to keep me awake; I drank several cups while I read a book I'd thrown into the bag—Clifford Irving's account of how he and Susskind attempted to pull off the hoax of the century by concocting a phony biography of Howard Hughes. I suspected that Irving was a bit of a shit, but he was a good writer with a great story to tell. I read until the book fell out of my hands.

11

On two new tyres, with a new windscreen and bacon, eggs, grilled tomato and toast inside me, I got to Campbelltown at 12.30, in time to catch Kathy coming off her shift. She still looked downcast but my judgment was that she was on the way up out of it. She had a naturally buoyant nature of a kind that's hard to keep down. We walked through the campus to the newspaper office, housed in a demountable building that had that resigned, permanent look they get when there's no money to replace them.

The *Southwestern Star* had a room in the building it shared with a student employment service, a textbook exchange and the Asian Students' Association. The room was small, lined with shelves crammed with books, newspapers, magazines and academic periodicals. The desk was a chaos of paper, audio cassettes, computer discs and plastic coffee cups, some bristling with pens and pencils. Kathy waved her hand at the mess apologetically.

'A lot of this's Mark's personal gear. It's all mixed in with the paper stuff. He wasn't a very organised person.'

At least she could speak his name without a sob and refer to him in the past tense. She'd get there. She sat down at the computer, turned it on and did the things young people can do—used the mouse, shot through all the intermediate stuff that baffles me and got what she wanted in seconds.

'Here it is. Notes on possible sources of steroids. This is all about what happened to Angela, of course. That was the password he used for this stuff. Angie. I was just fooling around and tried it and got in. It looks as if he had a . . . what d'you call it? Someone who knows things, in Sydney?'

'An informant.'

'That's right. There's a few code names in all this. Was he just being mysterious or what?'

'Hard to say. Investigative reporters do that.'

'That's right. That's what he said he wanted to be—an investigative reporter.' She sighed and tapped some keys. 'Anyway, it's hard to follow but . . . Jesus!'

The screen went blank.

'What's happened?'

She tapped keys frantically. 'I don't know. Oh, shit, yes, of course!'

'What?'

'He must've used a double password and put in a wipe function.'

'What's that?'

'It's a way of safeguarding files. He built in a second password and unless the user puts it in at some point the files get wiped. I'm sure that's what happened. Shit! I should have thought of it.

He was up to all the tricks that way. I'm sorry, Mr Hardy.'

I was sorry as well but I could hardly blame her. I scarcely understood what she was saying. 'Would the information be on the discs?'

'Maybe.' She pointed at the twenty or thirty discs littering the desk. 'But where would you start? And he would *definitely* have put massive protection on the discs. I wouldn't be able to get in. Oh, bugger him. Why'd he have to be so fucking clever?'

I had a feeling she was coming apart again. I spun her chair away from the computer, away from the source of her distress, away from Mark.

'Listen, Kathy. Don't worry. We'll be right. Now, there's obviously a way to make coffee around here. How's it work?'

'Jug in the employment centre. We all put in for the coffee and that.'

'Okay. I'm going to make some. White with three sugars, right?'

'Yes.'

Oh, to be young, I thought. 'Okay. Make your mind a blank. Back in a tick.'

The door to the employment centre was closed but not locked. I boiled the jug, took two plastic cups from the stack, spooned in the International Roast and added long-life milk and sugar to Kathy's and stirred. I took mine black.

'Here you go,' I said. 'Drink a bit. Mind a blank?'

She was close to tears. 'I feel an idiot getting you here . . . '

'That's not blank.'

'Okay. Blank. Might as well be.'

We sipped coffee for a few minutes. She put her cup down and moved as if to turn back to the computer but I stopped her.

'No. Listen. You read the stuff through once, didn't you?'

'Yeah. Sort of.'

'So it's a matter of what you can remember of it.'

She laughed and sounded as if she went on laughing she'd reach hysteria. That was the last thing I wanted. I shuddered at the thought of having to slap a young female student out of a fit when we were all alone in a demountable building at lunchtime. But she pulled back and suddenly seemed genuinely amused. Mood swings.

'You know I told you I was a lousy student?'

I nodded.

'That's mainly why. I've got a rotten memory.'

I shook my head. 'I don't believe it. Now, did Mark list some gyms or places that sold steroids?'

She nodded.

'You saw the names on the screen?'

Another nod.

'What were they?'

She shook her head. 'It's a waste of time. I haven't a clue. I wasn't concentrating on the detail. I was just, you know, interested, and then I thought about you and how Mark would've wanted me to help you. And now I've buggered it all up.'

I wanted to touch her, to comfort her, but these days you can't do that. 'Shush, Kathy. It's okay.'

'It's not fucking okay. Stop saying that. I've fucked up the way I always do. Why did I bother when all he wanted to do was screw that black . . . oh, god. Listen to me. You're wasting your time. All I can fucking remember from that bullshit is . . . '

'Yes, Kathy. What?'

She looked at me with tears running down her face and misery making her almost ugly. 'The informant. He was called Tank. I remember because it was such a funny name.'

'That's good. D'you know if it was a nickname for the bloke or one of Mark's code names?'

She shook her head. 'Don't know. I'm sorry.'

'Don't be. That's a big help.'

'Really?'

'Yes. Hang in there, Kathy. You're a hell of a lot better than you think you are.'

'Thank you, Mr Hardy. Will you let me know what happens? I mean about Clinton and everything?'

Looking ahead. Another good sign. I told her I'd keep in touch and I meant it.

As I left I kept an eye out for Tanya Martyn. Somehow I expected to see her sprinting by in her tracksuit or striding along in her short, tight skirt. I didn't and I was disappointed.

I drove home, washed some clothes, ate a late lunch and had an early drink and parked myself by the telephone. Two hours later I'd learned that the *Coral Queen* was registered to Rex Nickless. Mr Nickless was on the board of several corporations and the managing director of a company that constructed kit houses all over Australia and throughout the Pacific. Apparently Mr Nickless spent most of his time travelling about in his yacht inspecting the houses he'd supplied and built, preferably in exotic locations. He'd been married twice before and his current wife was Stella née Carfax, 31, a former air hostess.

Ocean-going boats were not obliged to report their courses or locations to the authorities but were strongly advised to do so. Nickless had state of the art communications equipment and followed the advice to the letter. He had registered with the New South Wales coastguard service and been placed on a schedule which required him to report his position at regular intervals. The service would not give me any specific information about his ports of call or dates of arrival and departure, but they did concede that the boat had travelled north and that Nickless most likely had made a similar arrangement with the Queensland authorities.

He had. For some reason the Queenslanders were more forthcoming. The *Coral Queen* had reported in from Stradbroke Island and other points up the coast including Fraser Island and had gone 'off schedule' at Port Douglas nine weeks previously. They couldn't, or wouldn't, give me any information about her whereabouts now.

I phoned the head office of Nickless Homes and asked to speak to the man himself. I was passed from pillar to post until I finally got Nickless' secretary who asked me the nature of my business. I told her I was a private detective working on a missing person case and that I believed Mr Nickless might be able to help me. I was put through to him as fast as the fibre-optic cables allowed.

'Mr Hardy is it? I understand you might have some information about my wife?'

That was encouraging. The voice was thin and strained with the rasp that comes from smoking thousands of cigarettes. 'Not exactly, Mr Nickless,' I said. 'But I'm sure we have something to talk about. I might mention the name George Cousins.'

'I want to see you straight away,' Nickless said. 'Right now. I'll pay you for your time. Please. I'm in Pyrmont.'

'I've got the address but it's after closing time. Your office . . . '

'Will be open, I assure you. Please come at once. I'll be waiting for you.'

12

Pyrmont has undergone a facelift and experienced a comeback recently. There's a nice mix of renovated business and residential buildings and the beginnings of a community life—I mean places to eat and drink and talk, especially drink. There'll never be much in the way of public space and the air quality will never be good, but that applies to a lot of Sydney. The cityscape makes it better looking at night than in the daytime, but the transport arrangements are good and property prices will rise and rise. I knew people who squatted there in the old days and some who paid laughably low rents. Not any more.

The office of Nickless Homes Inc. Pty Ltd was in Harris Street. The block had the Dunkirk Hotel at one end and the Duke of Edinburgh at the other. There were newly planted plane trees along one side, an outdoor cafe with chrome tables, a vegetarian eatery and Thai restaurant, giving the street a sophisticated, cosmopolitan look. The traffic was thin at that hour but would be heavy for most of the day. Parking space minimal.

The company's office was in a renovated three-storey terrace, one of several in the street that had been turned over to business. That seemed a bit incongruous to me until I got inside and discovered that one of their models was an artful reproduction of the classical Victorian terrace. I was met at the heavy glass security door by a young woman who took me up two flights of stairs to the executive area. The two bottom floors seemed to be where the work was done. The various home styles were depicted in elegant blown-up photographs beside the stairs and on the landings. Some were up on stilts, Queensland style, others were rambling affairs on slabs. There was the terrace, there were yurts and even a tree house. That amused me and I laughed.

'Sir?' the woman said.

'The tree house.'

'It's very popular. Mr Nickless said you were to go right in.'

Rex Nickless might not have looked too impressive on the jetty down at Bingara in shorts and deck shoes, but he looked the part in a suit behind a big teak desk in his flash office with big windows affording a magnificent city view. He got up as soon as I walked in the door and came quickly towards me around the desk, hand out.

'Mr Hardy. Thanks for coming so quickly.'

We shook and I got a surprise. He was small to medium sized, soft in the middle with receding hair and an advancing double chin, but his hand was hard and rough. This was a man who'd done a lot of manual work in his time. His blue eyes were clear and his skin was good. He looked his age but as if he had a few useful years left in him. I accepted his invitation to sit down in a leather chair and saw no reason not to also accept his offer of a drink. He operated the bar efficiently and put a solid Scotch on the rocks in my hand. He took his mineral water back behind the desk.

'Used to drink like a fish when I was a builder's labourer,' he said. 'Six-pack at lunch and a couple at the smokos. Knocked it off a few years ago, apart from an occasional blow-out.'

'Slow and steady, that's me,' I said.

'I admit I did a bit of a quick check on you after I got your call. Asked around. The consensus is you're good at what you do. I like that. I'm good at what I do as well.'

The sun was going down and the view behind him was starting to take on a Hollywood glow. The Scotch was top of the range and under the right circumstances I could've just sat there and enjoyed everything. Instead, I made some sort of modest reply and suggested that we get to the point.

'I think I can put some business your way,' Nickless said.

'Hold on. Not so fast. We've got a bit of ground to cover first.'

'You're right. I'm anxious. I won't beat around the bush. You're looking for George Cousins. So am I.'

'I know why I'm looking for him. I don't know why you are or if our interests are the same.'

'Good point. What else can it be but some criminal matter? Cousins kidnapped my wife. Or at least I thought he did. I paid a ransom of fifty thousand dollars.'

I looked around the office—expensive carpet, polished wood, Swedish furniture. I tasted the Scotch—single malt, no change out of ninety bucks for a bottle.

'Not that much for a wife for a man in your healthy financial state.'

He sighed. 'You're right. It was all very fishy from the start. Hold on.' He broke off and hit a button on his intercom. 'You can go, Nadine. Thanks. See you tomorrow.'

I drank some more Scotch and waited. I wasn't impatient. It amuses me to watch people deal with their overheads.

Nickless drained his mineral water, loosened his tie. 'Fuck it,' he said. 'I'll join you.'

He topped me up from a bottle with a label I didn't recognise and poured himself a solid jolt. He took a swig and seemed more relaxed immediately. 'Okay, it was like this. I hired Cousins as a deckhand . . . '

'In Bingara, couple of months ago.'

He raised his glass, signifying agreement. 'Right. Well, I thought Stella really didn't like Cousins, especially when he turned up all cut and bruised the way he did. I was wrong. Last to know and all that crap. The long and the short of it's this. We went up the coast and called in at places where our houses have been built—Byron Bay, Stradbroke Island, Noosa and north. Stella and I were getting along all right. I know I'm a mug, redneck like me marrying a beautiful woman, but I wasn't a complete mug.'

'I don't follow.'

'You'll see. Anyway, we got to Port Douglas and Stella went shopping and disappeared. Then I got a note saying that if I wanted to see her again I had to cough up fifty thousand. The envelope also contained some of her hair and big bits of her fingernails, like they'd been cut off right down. Stella was very proud of her nails. That got to me and I paid up. As you say, I can find that kind of money without too much trouble. Well, Stella turned up, all distressed and hysterical and Cousins vanished like smoke. A doctor sedated Stella and we flew back to Sydney. Two days later she was gone again and she's hired a high-price lawyer to handle the divorce. I reckon they were in it together.'

I shook my head. 'It's not clear to me.'

Nickless finished his drink, thought about another, decided against. 'We had a prenuptial agreement that limited what claims Stella could make on me if we split up. She'd get bugger-all really. She had no money except what I gave her. Suddenly, she can afford an up-market lawyer. Where'd she get the money?'

'He might be doing it on a contingency basis.'

'He isn't. I checked. He's been paid a fair bit up front. Now I'm going to have to negotiate because those prenuptial things aren't watertight. She's going to take me for a fair swag. Okay, more fool me. But I've got a good bloke on my side and I'll wear whatever it costs me within reason. Stella's a greedy bitch, but I knew that. Also she's too dumb to have worked the scheme out. What sticks with me is Cousins' part in it. He dreamed it up and they shared the money.'

'You're guessing.'

'Yeah, but I'm guessing right. Anyway, he can keep the bloody money. What I want is a statement from him that Stella was in on it with him. That'll give me some leverage when we get around the table with the fucking lawyers.'

I was thinking fast. It sounded as if I'd have to go to North Queensland to track Clinton and I didn't want to finance that myself. When it had all seemed reasonably close to home, I'd considered getting Wesley to re-hire me, although there were problems with that. Nickless' problem suggested another avenue. If a statement was all he wanted from Clinton, that wasn't inconsistent with my original brief simply to find him. It all depended on whether Nickless could be trusted, or managed.

'What do you say?' Nickless said.

'About what?'

'About me hiring you to find Cousins. You're already looking for him anyway so you can double dip. I'll pay your going rate and I won't be mingy on expenses and so on.'

'Good to hear,' I said. 'I'm tempted, but I've got an ethical problem.'

'What's that?'

'D'you mean what *is* an ethical problem or what's my specific one?'

'Don't patronise me, Hardy. I know I came up through the school of hard knocks but I know what an ethical problem is. What's yours?'

'Sorry, I was really just buying time to think. Your assumption that I was looking for the man you call Cousins on a criminal matter was wrong. My original client is simply concerned about his welfare. The fact is, I took the investigation as far as I could and reported a no-show. Then I got another lead that looked promising and I followed it up off my own bat. It brought me to you. Strictly speaking, I haven't got another client now.'

'Then what's the problem?'

'None, or not a big one, if you're fair dinkum that you're not going to lay charges.'

'You've got my word on it. I've told you what I want and that's it. I certainly don't want to have anything to do with fucking courts. Let's have another drink.'

I was going to have to taxi home if I accepted but how often did I get a chance to drink a single malt? Besides, I was beginning to like Nickless and not just on account of his whisky. I held out my glass and got another solid measure. He forgot about the ice this time. But to like is not necessarily to trust, and I didn't know whether to believe him absolutely. He was a difficult man to read with his soft belly and hard hands. I doubted that you could get as far as he had in the building game, especially starting from the bottom, if you were soft at the centre.

'You married, Hardy?'

'Was once.'

'Third time for me this was. You'd reckon I'd learn. I hope I have. I've got a good business here. Makes money, employs people and provides something useful and environmentally acceptable.'

'Good for you.'

'I want to hang on to it. If Stella took me to the cleaners it'd all be at risk. That's the truth. Shit, I want to fight her for my pride's sake and for all sorts of selfish reasons, but it's not entirely selfish.'

The whisky was going down like warm honey. 'I believe you.'

'I'm ready to lose the house. I've written that off. Never liked it much anyway. Her taste, not mine. But I don't want all this crap to cripple a good business I've worked like a dog to create.'

I believed him but I knew a bit about men like Nickless and some of the prints on the wall were a giveaway. 'What about the boat?'

He blinked nervously several times, looked at me and took a drink, a big one. 'Yeah, right. I don't want to lose the *Coral Queen*. I love that boat.'

Like the rest of us, the rich have their soft spots Different things, but they make them just as vulnerable. I nodded and finished my drink.

Nickless turned what was left of his around in his big, meaty hands. 'Can we come to terms then?'

'What were you going to do about Cousins if I hadn't shown up?'

He shrugged. 'Nothing. I had no idea what to do.'

'Okay, I think we can work something out. I'll need to talk to your wife.'

He snorted. 'I wish you luck. She's in London, doing it all by remote control.'

'Then I'll have to go to Queensland. Track him back from there. It'll be expensive.'

He shrugged. 'Not as expensive as if I've got no cards to play with. What're your rates?'

I told him and he wrote a cheque that would finance my trip to Queensland in style. I felt vaguely guilty as I folded it and tucked it away. I didn't know whether I'd be able to persuade Clinton Scott to do what Nickless wanted, even if I found him. I was flying by the seat of my pants and more concerned about seeing a job through and getting back on good terms with Wesley than with Nickless' problem. I hadn't resolved my ethical problem at all.

After leaving Nickless I went for a walk through Pyrmont to sober up and stimulate thought. There was a lot of dust in the air from building sites and the considerable revamping going on around Union Street. But the breeze from Darling Harbour was moving it around in true Sydney fashion. In this city you take the significant rough with the much greater smooth. I sobered up and did a lot of thinking, but I was already on my way to the sunshine state.

13

It wasn't the best time of the year to visit north
Queensland—too late, too hot, too sticky—but I
was able to afford air-conditioned motels and cars
and that would make all the difference. Swimming
pools would help as well, along with gins and
tonic, fresh fish with chilled wine and top quality
insect repellent. I booked on a midday Qantas
flight to Cairns with the comfortable feeling of
knowing that the cheques I'd posted had given
me plenty of clearance on my credit cards. Plus I
had cash in my pocket. I packed summer clothes
and, although I'd recently regained my permit to
carry a weapon—a right I'd lost as a result of
serving the short prison sentence some time
back—I left the Smith & Wesson at home. The
rigmarole of taking a gun on a domestic flight isn't
worth it, and you can always get a gun in Queensland if you know where to look.

I cancelled the paper delivery and asked my
neighbour Clive, a taxi driver who works irregular
hours like me, to collect my mail and keep an eye
on the house. Clive has a length of lead pipe
bound with insulating tape under the driver's seat

of his cab. Just what you want in a house-minder.

Cairns was windless, overcast and hot, but the tropical smell lifted my spirits. It's hard to say why. After my stint in Malaya I swore I'd never go north of Coffs Harbour again, but that passed and I feel a sense of freedom up north. People and things move more slowly and the air's better. I rented a Pajero with all the trimmings and got on the road to Port Douglas. The road was good and the Pajero handled well. I was passed by several stretch limos but felt no envy. I found Radio National and half-listened to a program about the El Niño effect as I admired the greenery. I've always liked palm trees and I don't mind a sugar-cane field either.

Port Douglas retains some of the features of the fishing village it once was, even though millions of dollars have been poured into it. As far as I could see, the renovations, restorations and new buildings had kept the north Queensland emphasis on timber, glass and tin and there were no high-rise monstrosities in sight. My expenses didn't run to the Mirage resort, where Christopher Skase is said to have spent a million dollars just on palm trees to line the drive. Well, it wasn't his money.

Just for fun I'd picked up the Mirage brochure at the airport—golf course and driving range, tennis courts, acres of swimming pools and three five-star restaurants. I booked into a motel with a swimming pool and a restaurant without stars. The minibar was well stocked and the air-conditioning worked, all I needed. I didn't play golf, wouldn't have time for tennis and twenty metres of swimming pool was enough for me.

After a swim and a shower I changed into shorts, sneakers and T-shirt and began the rounds, showing Clinton's photo down at the waterfront, in the pubs and shops, at the real estate agencies and car rental outfits. Over the next few days, I talked to white people and black people and Asians and mixes of all three, males and females, gays and straights, the drunk and the sober. I talked to a wary, suspicious policeman and to some women in a very welcoming establishment where I could've blown my expenses in no time flat.

I picked up his trail at a used car yard where he'd bought an ancient 4WD for a song.

'That's him,' the owner said. 'Bit rougher, but that's him all right. What's he done?'

'Run away from home. How'd he pay?'

He rubbed his thumb and forefinger together. 'In cash, mate, in cash.'

'Did he show you any ID? Did you see his licence?'

'No need. Cash transaction. Vehicle was registered. All above board.'

'What name did he use?'

'George.'

'Was he alone?'

'Yup.' He shifted his feet uncomfortably. 'Look, mate I've got things to do ... '

'Last thing. Did he say where he was going?'

'Said he was going bush.'

I got the registration number of the Land Rover

and a description—khaki and black, roof-rack, bullbars—and went to a large barn of a place that supplied building materials and camping gear. They remembered George. A young black guy who'd helped him load his purchases remembered the vehicle in detail.

'Fuckin' bomb. I told him it wouldn't get him fuckin' far but he didn't pay no notice. Nice bloke, though. Asked me a few questions about the language and stuff, you know. I know fuck-all about that shit. Tell you what, he had a ton of grog on board and lots of tucker—cans and packets and that.'

'Did he have maps?'

'Think so, yeah.'

'Of what?'

He shrugged. 'Search me.'

Back at the motel I took Roger, the proprietor, into my confidence. I'd eaten at his restaurant, made liberal use of his minibar and praised his swimming pool; he was mine. I explained my mission to him and produced a few maps I'd bought where 'George' had most likely bought his.

'All I've been told is that he was going bush and he had camping and cooking gear and plenty of supplies. Where d'you reckon he'd go, Rog?'

Rog studied the maps and chewed over the question very slowly. 'Blackfeller, you say?'

'Yes. No, not an Aborigine. West Indian. Like the cricketers.'

'Oh yeah? Well, I can't see why he'd go bush. Head for a beach more likely.'

111

I thought about Danny Roberts and Clinton's day in the bush and how Clinton had pressed for information and was upset at not getting it. He was on some kind of quest and I had the feeling he'd carry on with it up here.

I shook my head. 'I think the bush'd be right. Say he's on some kind of survival kick. Where would he go?'

'He's a smart bloke?'

'Pretty smart.'

He put his finger on the map. 'I reckon he'd head for the Daintree National Park. Very rugged up there, rough as you like, but you can get help if you need it. Should have a permit, but.'

'I doubt he'd bother with that.'

'The rangers'd spot him eventually then, but he could get himself pretty well lost in there for a while. Does he fish?'

He had a good teacher, I thought. 'Yeah.'

'Plenty of fish. He'd have to carry a lot of fuel. So will you if you're going in after him, Cliff. And I'd advise you to talk to the rangers first.'

'Right, I will. Thanks Rog.'

I didn't talk to the rangers, but I did load up on fuel, wet and dry supplies and camping gear. As I stuffed the tent in next to the primus stove I smiled at the thought of what my city friends would say if they saw me. I was no fan of ground-sheets and guy ropes. Didn't like damper. I was notorious for preferring pavements to paddocks, beaches to the bush. *To hell with them*, I thought and went out and bought a pair of Rossi boots and an Akubra hat. At Rog's suggestion, I bought a couple of cartons of cigarettes. According to Rog, smokes could buy you useful cooperation in the bush. I hadn't bought cigarettes for years and wondered if I'd be able to resist temptation when I was sitting at my camp fire with a belly full of tinned stew and an enamel mug of Bundy rum in my hand.

I knew it was a crazy thing to do, head off into a wilderness area with only a guess to go on. I rationalised it to myself by thinking that the kid at the hardware store would be right and that the decrepit Land Rover wouldn't make it to the Daintree. But in reality I was indulging myself at a rich man's expense. I could keep a log of my travels, report on information received, play at going bush myself. Why not? The way my life was at the moment, any change, any diversion from the tried and tested routines was welcome. With Glen Withers married, Cy Sackville dead and Frank Parker retired from the police, I had a sense of a phase of my life slipping past me. It wasn't anything like tragic, but it wasn't altogether comfortable either. I could treat this trip as a kind of emotional divide between the old comforts and what lay ahead.

But I didn't entirely rule out the possibility that I might actually find Clinton Scott sitting under a tree in the rainforest.

I didn't find him although I'd set out on the right track. The country and my inexperience defeated me but I had some luck. I had a few days wandering around the fringes of the national park, camped and coped pretty well with the rough roads, the heat, the insects, the sun, the rain and damp wood. I resisted the lure of tobacco but used the Bundy to put me to sleep in the noisy bush nights. I asked people about the Land Rover and a few claimed to have seen it. I gave them cigarettes. Eventually I entered the national park and was stopped by a ranger within two days.

He told me I was facing a fine and confiscation of my vehicle. I told him my story and showed him my credentials. He was unimpressed. He searched the Pajero for drugs and firearms and looked disappointed when he found only alcohol and tobacco. We stood by our vehicles, two big men in shorts, boots and wide-brimmed hats. He was coming across as tough but something told me that it was partly an act. After a while I sensed what it was, he was lonely.

'Look,' I said. 'I know I'm in the wrong and what I've done is dopey. I'll pay the fine. No worries. But I've got a distraught father on my back and I'm trying to do something for him. Are you a father?'

He took off his hat and scratched at where the sweat had matted his hair to his scalp. 'Yeah, I am. Two boys. Not that I get to see 'em that much.'

'Well, you understand what this bloke's going through. His boy's just disappeared up here.'

'Old Land Rover?'

I nodded and recited the registration number.

'She caught on fire.'

114

'Jesus. What happened to the driver?'

He wiped the sweatband on his hat with the tail of his shirt and put the hat back on. 'Follow me,' he said.

I learned a bit about 4WD driving over the next hour. The ranger seemed to be able to miss all the bumps I'd been hitting and I finally picked up the knack of reading the slopes and ruts in such a way as to anticipate the next trouble spot and avoid it. He kept up a good pace and several times had to stop to allow me to catch up. I was dripping with sweat when we finally pulled up at a small settlement by a creek. It consisted of nine or ten fibro, tin-roofed houses dotted around a two-acre clearing. There were fenced, bird-proofed garden beds, gravel paths and clothes lines strung between trees. Two 4WDs parked in the shade looked serviceable, three others nearby looked as if they were cannibalised to keep the others running.

Half a dozen Aboriginal children were playing by the creek, some women were working in the gardens. I saw no men. The ranger climbed down and gestured for me to do the same.

'Abo reserve, this,' he said. 'The men're off working or hunting, most of 'em. But the old bloke should be round. Go easy. They don't like whitefellers, especially blokes who look like you 'n' me.'

'Why're we here?'

'You'll see.'

We crunched up a path to one of the houses and waited until a woman working in a garden nearby came over to us. The ranger took off his hat and I did the same.

'Tommy around, Mrs Palmer?'

'Should be, Mr Lewis. Reckon he's down by the creek teachin' the kids somethin' or other.'

'Thank you.'

Lewis restored his hat to his head and we moved off. 'Get some of those smokes you've got in your vehicle,' he said. 'Couple of packets. Tommy loves a smoke.'

I got the cigarettes and we began to walk towards the creek. We were still almost a hundred metres away when a figure seemed to rise out of the ground and move towards us. It moved slowly, bent over to one side.

Lewis chuckled. 'One of the kids must've spotted us. Tommy'd try to tell you that he saw our faces in the water or in the clouds, but that's all bullshit.'

'What's the matter with him?'

'He's old. Christ knows *how* old. He was a stockman for donkey's years. Needs a hip replacement.'

I wondered whether he'd get it. 'This looks like a well-run place.'

'It is. They run it themselves. Never any trouble here. Two rules—no whitefeller religion and no grog. They're very strong on the old ways. The boys get initiated and all that. Fucking cruel if you ask me, but that's the way they want it. Seems to work. No petrol sniffers here, mate.'

The old man limping towards us stopped and we had to go the extra yards to reach him. I thought that was a pretty good strategy for getting the upper hand. Tommy was very, very old. What little hair he had was white and his thick beard was the same except where it had been stained by nicotine. He had been tall but age and injuries had shrunken him. One eye was milky with cataract, the other looked all right. He was rail thin in his clean denim shorts and army shirt.

'Gidday, Tommy,' Lewis said. He didn't take off his hat or offer to shake hands.

'Mr Lewis. Who's that with you?'

'Names's Hardy,' Lewis said. 'City bloke.'

In my shorts, sweat-stained work shirt, three-day stubble and boots, topped off by my Akubra, I thought this description a bit unkind but Tommy nodded as if he could see beneath the surface of things to the essential man within. Still, he was guarded.

'Gidday.'

I felt that old uncertainty. He had a lot of poise and there was wisdom in the ancient, lined face. I didn't feel entitled to address him as Tommy so I just nodded and gave him a wary smile.

'Quiet bloke,' Tommy said. 'He all right, Mr Lewis?'

'Dunno,' Lewis said. 'You judge.'

None of my contact with city blacks was going to do me any good here. I felt uncomfortable, ambivalent. The ban on booze and Christianity seemed sensible but I wasn't so sure about the ritual cutting and slicing. The old Aborigine read me right.

'I'd say he was a thoughtful bloke, Mr Lewis,'

Tommy said, sticking out a gnarled hand. 'Call me Tommy.'

I shook a hand as hard and strong as mulga wood.

Lewis cleared his throat. 'Like to have a bit of talk, Tommy, about that feller your blokes pulled out of the burning Land Rover a while back. Hardy here's looking for him.'

'George,' Tommy said. 'He in trouble?'

I shook my head. 'Not from me. His family's worried about him. His father hired me to look for him.'

The old man moved forward a few steps to get himself into the shade. 'Sons,' he said. 'I had six of 'em. Grog killed three, one hung himself in gaol, one's here an' he's all right. Dunno about the other. They're a handful, sons. George's father's right to be worried.'

'Why d'you say that?'

'Payback,' Tommy said.

14

That knocked for six the comfortable theory I'd been forming—that Clinton's obsession with Aborigines had taken over from his thirst for revenge. We went into one of the houses and a woman made us tea. The house was sparsely furnished but neat and clean and the teapot and mugs had seen a lot of service. We sat at an old pine table and I shared around the cigarettes, managing to leave the packets on the table. What relation the woman, whose name was Beth, was to Tommy I never discovered, but she was obviously a person of influence in the community and had had a fair bit to do with 'George'. First, they wanted to know everything I knew before Tommy would expand on his statement and their questions were canny and to the point. I told them almost everything, leaving out Nickless' suspicions about the kidnapping conspiracy.

'He was a good boy, that George,' Beth said.

I didn't want a hymn of praise, I wanted observations and pointers to behaviour. 'I'm told he was a bit of a drinker,' I said.

'No drink here,' Beth said. 'Not allowed. George

didn't seem to miss it and he was here a couple of weeks.'

I thought about the rum and wine in my Pajero and hoped none of the kids went poking about. 'Was he badly burned in the fire?'

'Pretty bad,' Tommy said. 'Body burns mostly but Beth here was a nurse and we've got a pretty good supply of medicine and that.'

'Our people always got burned a lot,' Beth said. 'The way we lived it couldn't be helped. And the boozers were always setting themselves on fire. I know a few bush treatments for burns. George come up all right with a bit of blackfeller as well as whitefeller medicine.'

'So he didn't have to stay as long as he did?'

Tommy and Beth looked at each other. My question had pushed us past the formalities into the territory of real information.

'Not a lot I can tell you ... ' Tommy began, stubbing out a cigarette.

I pushed a packet towards him. 'I know he was very interested in traditional Aboriginal life and the languages and so on. I've talked to a Koori bloke down south who said George grilled him about that. And a young fellow at the camping goods store in Port Douglas told me the same.'

'That's right,' Tommy said. 'He asked a lot of questions and I gave him a few answers. Only a few, mind.'

'I understand,' I said. 'A man with a West Indian father and white mother's practically a white man.'

Tommy smiled and opened his hands, the cigarette held between his twisted fingers. 'Sort of.

120

But I told him a few things and Beth did the same.'

She nodded. 'He talked to me about the black girl who died. Wanted to know if we believed that the dead live on, that stuff, you know.'

'What did you tell him?'

'I can't tell you.'

Lewis had been quiet, smoking his share of the cigarettes with the other two. Now I could sense his impatience and knew I had to hurry things along.

'Tell me about the payback, Tommy. I know something of what he had in mind, but ... '

Tommy sucked smoke deep into his lungs and let it out through his nose as he spoke. 'Tried to talk him out of it. Told him he was headed for trouble but he wouldn't listen. He reckoned he was going to find the people who'd killed his woman and kill them.'

'How?'

I meant how was he going to find them, but Tommy took it a different way. 'With a spear or an axe,' he said.

'Did he say where he'd find them?'

'Sydney.'

'Any names?'

Tommy looked at Beth who shook her head. He put out his cigarette and moved the stubs round in the saucer that served as an ashtray. 'No names. But I reckon he knew who he was after or had a good idea. I'd say he held that back from me the way I held stuff back from him, you know?'

I nodded. It was convincing if unhelpful. Beth slapped at a fly and Lewis shifted his feet again. Time was running out fast. 'Just one thing I have to ask,' I said. 'Did he have any money?'

They both looked at Lewis, who took another cigarette and lit it with the disposable lighter I'd left on the table. 'Nothin' to do with me,' he said.

Beth, who was a tall, stout woman wearing a flowing cotton dress, stood and ran her hands around her protuberant middle. 'He wore a money belt thing around here. He paid me for everything he'd eaten and for the creams I'd used and some more besides. We need it and I took it.'

'And where did he go?'

Tommy studied me for a minute before he spoke. 'You talk him out of that payback stuff if you find him?'

'Yes.'

'Got a lift into Mossman.'

'Thank you,' I said. 'I'd say he was very lucky to find you.'

'My oath,' Lewis said, getting to his feet. 'And I reckon you might say the same.'

'Could I make some sort of contribution to . . . '

Beth flared. 'We're not a charity.'

'I know. I just wanted to show some appreciation for your help. The boy's father'd want me to do that, too.'

'I dunno,' Tommy said.

'Look, I've got some camping gear out there that I won't be needing any more. There's a tent and some groundsheets, a primus with a couple of bottles of fuel, jerry cans and stuff. I'm sure you could make some use of it. Otherwise I'll just have to dump it or sell it for a song.'

'Thanks,' Beth said. 'Yeah, that'd be good.'

I shook hands with her and we trooped out to my 4WD. I did the unloading, shoving things around so as to conceal the grog but Tommy spotted it and winked his clouded eye at me. 'Useta be a demon on the rum,' he said.

I handed him a carton of cigarettes. 'I believe you. These things'll kill you, you know.'

'Haven't yet.'

We shook and he shouted for some kids to come and carry the gear away under his supervision. They were healthy and strong. A little ten-year-old lifted the box carrying the enamel plates and mugs, a bush knife and a tomahawk, a gas bottle and a big can of motor oil onto his shoulder with ease and trotted away with it.

'Nice touch that, Hardy,' Lewis said. 'I suppose you'll be heading for Mossman.'

'That's right. And thanks for your help.'

'S' orright. Any idea of how to get there?'

'I've got some maps.'

'Bugger that. Look, I'll show you.'

He picked up a stick and began to scratch marks in the sandy soil. I nodded as he talked about east and west and how many kilometres one place was from another. I've forgotten my army training and have trouble with the points of the compass and still think in miles. I nodded and grunted affirmatively, but none of it made sense to me. Lewis noticed and rubbed out the hieroglyphics.

123

'Fuck it, I'll put you on the way. Give us a smoke for the road.'

I opened my hands. 'They've all gone.'

'That'd be right.'

We set off. Some of the kids ran alongside us for longer than you'd imagine, keeping up better than you'd think possible. Eventually they dropped off and stood waving. I waved my arm out of the window until the next turn in the track. Lewis drove fast, threw up a lot of dust and it took a lot of concentration to keep in touch with him. He was testing me, showing me who was boss and I just had to cop it. I'd probably have done the same in his place. My shirt was a wet rag clinging to my body when Lewis stopped at a crossroad. He pointed, made sure I'd seen the direction, and drove off.

There was a six-pack of Fourex in the back of the Pajero. I pulled in under a tree and drank two cans, scarcely taking a breath in between. I sat in the shade and looked out at the lush, green landscape. The air was barely moving but it seemed to carry a dozen different scents on it, none of which I recognised. Birds flew about and I couldn't identify any of them either, or the trees they inhabited. I realised just how citified I was and, although it was an uncomfortable feeling, it was way, way too late to do anything about it. The beer had made me sleepy and the last thing I wanted to do was fall asleep under a tree in the middle of nowhere. The insects would love that.

It was late in the afternoon but still hot. I

splashed cold water on my face, drank some, stuffed half a packet of chewing gum into my mouth and drove on in the direction indicated. I hadn't asked Lewis how far it was and was thinking of consulting my map when a few buildings appeared on the horizon and another vehicle overtook me. The driver waved and I waved back, mostly out of relief. The dirt gave away to bitumen and signs began to confirm that Mossman would be reachable before dark.

I was shocked at the state of the Pajero when I pulled in at the first motel I saw. The vehicle was covered in grey dust so its original colour was a matter of guesswork. No-one else gave it a second look. I checked in, unpacked minimally and spent an hour in the swimming pool. Not for the first time I looked at my stubble and contemplated a beard. A mature look, reliable. The grey I saw among the black decided me against it.

I had my usual motel dinner of biscuits, chips and nuts, two more beers and fell asleep. I dreamed I was cutting sugarcane in a huge field. It was the middle of the day and the sun was beating down fiercely. I could hear snakes rustling in the cane. A gang of kanakas arrived and I thought they were going to help but they stood around and smoked their clay pipes and laughed at me.

PART
TWO

15

I checked at the airport and railway and bus stations, showed Clinton's photo and didn't get a whiff of him. Likewise at the wharf. I wasn't surprised. He could have bought another car, but I wasn't going to spend time on that possibility. He might've hitchhiked out for all I knew. All my enquiry told me that he was gone and that was all I really needed to know. I drove back to Cairns and handed over the Pajero, after putting it through a car wash and cleaning it out a bit inside. I kept the maps. I could plot my movements on them as further evidence for Nickless of my dedication to duty. I cursed myself for not getting the name of the Aboriginal settlement, then decided that it didn't matter. I'd been there and learned things, none of them useful to Nickless but possibly helpful to me.

I gave the Akubra to an Aboriginal kid working in the airport garden. I kept the boots. I had a last Fourex in the airport bar while waiting for the flight to Brisbane and read through the *Sydney Morning Herald* to see what I'd been missing. Not much. The Olympics were drawing closer and I was still tossing up whether to stay and go to the boxing and watch the marathon or give the whole thing a miss and spend the fortnight on Norfolk Island. No chance of tickets to the swimming or athletics and I wasn't sure I wanted to be around when the tourists flooded in. Some people said you could rent your house out for a fortune and others said you couldn't. I remained in two minds.

Divided loyalties make for uneasiness, as every adulterer knows. All the way back to Sydney, including the wait at Brisbane, while I was trying to read the Irving book I was really worrying about how I stood with Wesley Scott and Rex Nickless. Their interests weren't identical but not diametrically opposed either. Wesley stood on the higher moral ground. Nickless had paid for the Queensland trip which had yielded some things but nothing conclusive. My only way forward now was to pursue the clue Mark Alessio and Kathy Simpson had thrown up—the identity of 'Tank'—and that had arisen from my own, self-financed endeavours. I couldn't decide quite who I was working for, but I knew that Wesley deserved to know that his boy was still alive and relatively unharmed two months ago.

Sydney was warmish but it felt cool after Queensland. The air was lousy. Clive gave me my mail and said that no-one had tried to burgle my house. He sounded disappointed not to have had a chance to use his lead pipe. The mail was routine stuff and there was nothing pressing in the answering machine messages. There were a couple of small jobs on offer and I could deal with them while still pursuing Clinton Scott. I phoned Harry Tickener at *The Challenger* and asked him if anyone connected with sport had been killed in the last week or so.

'Not that I've heard of. A few should have been, of course, if there was any justice.'

Harry, a green baize fanatic, would be talking about professional snooker players who interested me about as much as synchronised swimmers.

'No gymnasium types, personal trainers, people like that?'

'What a weird question. Tried to call you a couple of days ago for a drink. Where've you been?'

'Queensland.'

'That explains it. They're all a bit light-sensitive up there.

I felt like arguing. There was nothing deficient about Roger, Beth, Tommy or Ranger Lewis, but I didn't bother. We arranged to meet for a drink in two days. I admired my tan under the shower and washed some clothes. I spent the evening cleaning my Rossis and knocking out an interim report on the word processor for Nickless. I still hadn't spent all of his money and I suspected that Clinton was in the same boat. I felt an odd bond with him. I told Nickless about the inflammable Land Rover and said that I'd picked up a few leads to pursue in Sydney. Half-true. Among my ragtail collection of books were a couple of paperbacks, acquired when I was a disenchanted law student thinking about switching to anthropology. I never made the switch. Kinship systems bored me as much as contract law. I browsed through A. P. Elkins' *The Australian Aborigines*, reading up on 'revenge killings' and 'revenge expeditions'.

The next morning, early, I presented myself at Wesley's gym. I took my program card from the rack and winced when I saw how long it had been since my last workout. Riding around in a 4WD in Queensland and drinking Bundaberg rum wouldn't have done anything for my fitness. I started off on the bike at a lower grade than when I'd last been and after fifteen minutes I was dripping. I moved onto the machines and, even though I reduced the weight stacks and the repetitions, I struggled.

The gym was busy with most of the machines in use and the basketball players occupying a lot of space. I saw Wesley emerge from the massage room but it was a while before he saw me. I was battling with the leg press and had to reduce the weight to get through the set. Wesley noticed and almost cracked a smile. I was a ruin when I finished but I didn't stint. I spent the full time on the most boring part of the business, stretching, looped my damp towel around my neck and approached Wesley. He was rubbing the shoulder of a footballer, a big area.

'Hello, Cliff. Been a while.'

'Every muscle in my body says so.'

'Yeah, man. You've softened up a bit.'

'I've got some news, Wes.'

His big, oiled hands stopped moving. 'Good news?'

'I think so. Yes.'

Wesley slapped the meaty shoulder. 'You'll do, Vince. Go easy for a week or so.'

Vince got up and worked the shoulder. 'Feels good, Wes. Thanks.'

Wesley nodded. 'Come inside, Cliff.'

We went into the massage room and he said, 'What?'

'I've met some people, Aborigines, who saw Clinton alive and well about seven weeks ago.'

Wesley sat down abruptly, almost missing the chair and having to fight for his balance. Clumsiness like that was unlike him. 'Jesus,' he said. 'Where was this?'

'In North Queensland.'

He reached for a towel to wipe his hands. 'I don't understand. You reported a dead end . . . '

I sat on the massage table and rotated my stiff, aching shoulders. 'Some more information came my way and I followed up on it. It led me to Queensland.'

'I thought you'd just quit on me.'

'I know you did.'

'I'm sorry, man. I'll pay you . . . '

'That's the tricky part, Wes. Someone else who wants to find Clinton hired me after I did a bit of poking about on my own. He went south at first, to Bingara. That's where Angela Cousins' mother's people come from.'

'Why is someone else looking for him?'

I intended to give him an edited version, but

when I tried to hedge he was shrewd enough to ask the right questions and I ended up giving him the complete story. No names though.

Wesley cracked his knuckles with a noise like firecrackers. 'You believe this guy only wants Clinton to make some sort of statement?'

'I don't know.'

'I doubt he'd do that, Clinton.'

'Me, too. But would you have thought he'd be part of a blackmail scam?'

Wesley shook his head. 'This guy, maybe he really wants to put Clinton in gaol? That'd really put the screw on his wife.'

I shrugged. 'I don't know, Wes. Maybe. I've got a conflict of interest here.'

'Not so. I don't care if he has to go to gaol for a while. Couldn't be that long. No-one got hurt if what you say's right and I can give back the money. But this payback stuff, that sounds dangerous as hell to me. You say he thinks the girl got the stuff in Sydney?'

I let out a long breath. Wesley had just resolved my dilemma. It looked as if I could have the luxury of playing straight with both him and Nickless. How Clinton would react was another matter. 'Right. And I've got a bit of a lead there that you can help me with if we can agree ... '

'Hang on. I've got to ring Mandy. She's been in a very bad way over this. Me too, and Pauline. You imagine the worst bloody things ... ' He grabbed the phone and made the call. There was a strength in his voice and confidence in his delivery. It must have communicated itself to his wife because there was a smile on his face when he hung up. 'Mandy says to thank you.'

'Okay, but it's a bit early for that.'

'You said you had a lead.'

'Yes, but it's sort of in your area of expertise, maybe. And I want you to agree to let me handle it, right up until I ask for your help.'

'Butt out in other words.'

'Not exactly. In fact I'm going to need some assistance right away.'

Wesley scratched at the bristle on his face which, I noticed, had a lot of grey in it, like mine. 'You know I paid the rent on that house in Helensburgh and the kid came up and thanked me. He got his degree all right. He also returned Clinton's car. I put it up on blocks in the garage at home. I guess that was a vote of confidence or something. You've given us hope, Cliff, and we're grateful. I'll do what you say, but I sure as shit wish I do get the chance to help you. I'm serious, man. Not being able to do anything is the worst part.'

It was time to take a stab at it. 'Fair enough,' I said. 'Here's where it starts. Do you know someone nicknamed Tank?'

'Of course I know him. Everyone in this game knows him. He's an American, ex-marine, ex-pro wrestler. Runs a gym in Zetland.'

'That right? I thought there were only factories in Zetland.'

Wesley shook his head. 'A few houses, mostly owned by Tank. And then there's his gym.'

'I need to talk to him. Mark Alessio had him

down as someone who might know where Angela got the steroids. There's a chance Clinton might be on the same trail.'

'I hope not.'

'Why's that? You think he could be source of the stuff?'

'No, he's not that dumb. But Tank Turkowitz is one of the nastiest bastards you'd ever hope to meet, or hope not to meet. He married an Australian girl to get residence and the word is he killed her a bit later. Nothing proven. He trains some athletes and footballers and basketballers but his big thing is training fighters for smokos—you know, the all-in bareknuckle brawls they hold in out of the way places.'

I'd heard of these events—brutal, no-holds-barred affairs that attracted the worst elements in the community of violence—washed-up boxers and footballers, street fighters, standover men, bouncers and the drug-pushers, gamblers and pimps that circled around them.

'It sounds like the right scene.'

'Man, you got it right,' Wesley said. 'If you're going to talk to Tank Turkowitz you need my help right now!'

'I don't want to fight him. I just want to talk to him.'

Wesley flicked the towel at me. His spirits were definitely up. 'With Turkowitz, Cliff, talking and fighting is much the same thing.'

16

Wesley said he'd ring Turkowitz to set up a
meeting and would get back to me with the
where and when. The workout had left me
stiff and sore. I went to the Leichhardt squash
centre and spent half an hour in the sauna
and spa and, as always, couldn't decide after-
wards whether I felt better or worse. I drove to
the office, made a neat package of the report,
the annotated maps and the receipts and mailed
the lot off to Rex Nickless. After doing the arith-
metic I discovered that there wasn't as much left
of his money as I'd thought. Somehow, that
made me feel better.

I spent the day attending to the minor matters
that only took phone calls and faxes to deal
with—a surveillance of a factory to be arranged
a month hence, a subpoena to be served and a
promise to meet a journalist to talk about a case
I'd handled three years ago, a promise I probably
wouldn't keep. While waiting for Wesley to call I
brought my personal case doodle up to date. This
is the diagram I draw which shows the names of
all the people involved and the connections

between them and sometimes stimulates thought and questions. I added Tank Turkowitz to the picture, connected him to Mark Alessio with an arrow and to Clinton Scott with a dotted line that indicated a possible connection. It all looked very nice. In theory, Turkowitz would tell me who'd supplied the steroids to Angela and I'd somehow find Clinton sniffing at the same trail and stop him. In theory. When I'd finished I was sorry that I'd made the diagram—I had to add too many question marks to feel confident about any of it.

Wesley phoned late in the afternoon to say that he had lined up a meeting with Turkowitz at his gym for 6.30 that evening.

I said, 'Should I bring my gun?'

'Don't joke. Bring your patience and forebearance and your capacity to be insulted without having to retaliate.'

'I always do that.'

'Hah. How's the body?'

'Sore.'

'Teach you not to neglect it. I'll meet you there. Here's the address.'

He gave it and I jotted it down. Zetland wasn't even a place to drive through in my experience, let alone one to visit unless you need something of a light industrial nature. On my way home I stopped at the library, looked it up in Ruth Park's guidebook to Sydney and discovered that it was named after an undistinguished aristocrat, the Earl of Zetland, who was a mate of one of the nineteenth-century governors. Undistinguished was appropriate.

138

I drew out some money thinking that it might help to soothe the beast if it turned savage, equipped myself with a small, lead-weighted cosh that snuggled into a jacket pocket and set out for Zetland. Wesley was already there when I arrived at 6.20, sitting in his old Volvo and listening to 'PM'. I rapped on the window and he wound it down.

'Go in early,' I said 'Advantage of surprise. Old private eye trick.'

'Bullshit. Mandy says we should call in the police—arrest you, arrest Tank, arrest Nickless, arrest everybody.'

'I don't think that's a good idea.'

'Neither does she. She's just anxious. I didn't tell her about the woman and the burns. It made the story kind of thin.'

'Let's try and firm it up.'

The gym was a converted factory—concrete surrounds, high-set windows, flat roof. A loading dock ran down one side of it and there were holes in the cement out front where a chain link fence had been removed to make way for cars to park. The nine or ten cars were a mixed lot, from a Merc and a souped-up Mini through several Japanese compacts down to a battered VW, identical to one I'd owned twenty years ago. There were no houses in the street, just factories and storage facilities, all quiet at this time of day.

We went in through an automatic-opening front door to a carpeted reception area where some money had been spent—grey paint, concealed lighting, pot plants, stairs with a polished rail to a mezzanine floor. Through another set of doors I could see gymnasium equipment under fluorescent light that bounced off the many mirrors around the walls.

'I don't see a boxing ring,' I said.

'There's a kind of bear pit out the back.

We approached a counter where a short man with no shoulders, no chin and no hair stood tapping a pencil on the surface in front of him.

'Members only,' he said.

Wesley fronted the desk and the physical differences between the two men made you wonder if they were of the same species. 'Wesley Scott. To see Tank.'

The man nodded and showed small, badly decayed teeth. 'He said to challenge you.'

'You did that,' Wesley said.

'Up the stairs, gents.'

We went up the staircase and Wesley knocked at the door that had a sign reading Manager on it.

I said, 'Manager?'

Wesley shrugged. 'Tank manages rather than owns for tax purposes.'

'Wise,' I said.

'As I told you, Tank isn't dumb.'

The door opened and a giant stood there, filling the space. He was over two metres tall and must have weighed more than 150 kilos. He stood in the doorway but his belly, enclosed in an immaculate lightweight suit, protruded out beyond it. His head was shaved and oiled and it and his neck made a continuous column down to shoulders like a wardrobe. Wordlessly, he opened his arms to embrace Wesley who stepped nimbly back.

'No way, Tank. I don't need any crushed ribs.'

'Wes, my man, I'm hurt.' The accent was heavy, a product of some part of New York City.

'You're not and neither am I. Tank, this is Cliff Hardy.'

I nodded and kept my hands in my pockets.

Turkowitz grinned, showing gold-filled teeth. He also had a diamond stud in one ear. 'Hi, Hardy. I see my man here has briefed you.'

I smiled and said nothing. I was glad to have his man along as my man. From the look of him, you could whale away at Turkowitz with your hands and feet and even your little cosh for an hour and he'd still break you in half.

'A bit of your time, Tank,' Wesley said.

'As much as you want.' Turkowitz stepped aside, waved us in and shot back his snowy French cuff to consult a gold Rolex. 'As long as it isn't more than fifteen minutes.'

The office was about as tastefully got up as you could manage in a space carved out of a factory. The carpet, desk and trophy cabinet were a hymn to past success and present prosperity. Turkowitz motioned us into chairs and sat behind his desk. He folded his massive hands on the surface in front of him. His manicured fingernails gleamed.

'What's goin' down, Wes? We goin' to arm wrestle or are you opening up a branch down the block?'

'Let's cut the bullshit, Tank. My son's missing. Hardy here's looking for him and his enquiry has sort of led him here.'

141

Turkowitz shook his head. 'Man, I didn't even know you had a son. Me, I've got five, or maybe six. I forget.'

'I'm not saying you know anything about Wes's son,' I said. 'Not directly. But you did meet a man called Mark Alessio.'

'Who says?'

'He did.'

Turkowitz raised his hand to his mouth as if he wanted to chew at a fingernail. He thought better of it, but the hand wavered uncertainly. 'He's dead, I heard. An' if he's been shooting his mouth off about me I ain't sorry.'

'He hasn't. He created some computer files about his investigation into how some athletes get hold of steroids. Your name's in the files as someone who could put the finger on the source. Specifically, some steroids used by a girl named Angela Cousins. The stuff killed her.'

'Dumb little shit. What's he doing writing stuff like that down?'

'All I want to know is what you told him.'

'And why you talked to him,' Wesley said.

'Second question's easy. Kid paid me. An easy two grand. Sold his fucking bike, he said.'

Wesley cracked the knuckles on one hand. 'Did you kill him, Tank?'

'Shit, no. But like I say, I might've if I'd known how loose his mouth was.'

'Don't worry,' I said. 'He built a code into his computer set up. The file with your name on it got wiped when we called it up a second time.'

Turkowitz's smile returned, complete with the

glinting gold and what I now saw as the glistening porcelain caps. Slowly, lovingly, he turned the diamond stud in his ear. 'Then you got no leverage,' he purred.

Wesley cracked the other set of knuckles.

'No,' I said. 'But I've got Wesley who's got a big vested interest.'

Turkowitz's hands were folded again, composed. He stared at me and then shifted his massive head fractionally to look at Wesley. 'Be interestin',' he said.

'Ten years ago, Tank,' Wesley said. 'Maybe. Not now.'

Turkowitz sighed. 'You're right. But I could whistle an' get me some heavy help.'

Wesley looked around the room and his gaze rested on the trophy cabinet which held, among other things, an ornate ceremonial sword. Turkowitz swivelled to see where he was looking.

'I hate to think of the damage that could be done here,' Wesley said. 'Me being a man of peace.'

The tension went out of Turkowitz's expression and body. He leaned back against his chair and it groaned in protest.

'You're a slob, Tank,' Wesley said.

Turkowitz's swarthy face darkened. A flush spread up to his bald head. 'Don't fuckin' push me, Wes. Right, I talked to the Alessio kid. I have to say he had balls, comin' in here like that. I told him who most likely gave the horse pills to this girl.'

'Horse pills?' I said.

Turkowitz waved me quiet. This was between

him and Wesley now. 'Manner of speakin'. I told
him Stan Morris.

It was Wesley's turn to relax. 'Morris being your
main rival in the all-in fighting business.'

Turkowitz shrugged. 'I heard all his blokes're
on the horse pills. Seemed likely.'

'How do I get in touch with Morris?' I said.
'Where does he live?'

Turkowitz flicked a finger at his desk calendar.
'I don't rightly know and I don't know nobody
who does. Moves around, I guess. Just so happens
though, there's a smoko tomorrow night out
Badgerys Creek way. I've got a boy up in the main
event and so has Stan. You could try your luck
there.'

'Is that what you told Mark Alessio?'

Turkowitz nodded. 'Same thing. Sent him to a
smoko down south. Albion Park, around there.'

'You wouldn't tip Morris off about Hardy would
you, Tank?'

'Fuck, no. I wouldn't tip Stan Morris off if there
was a truck about to hit him.'

'Okay,' Wesley said. 'And . . . '

Turkowitz crinkled his forehead. 'What?'

'Come on, Tank. The password.'

'Oh yeah, almost forgot. Password's "rust".'

It was Wesley's turn to look surprised. 'Rust?
Why?'

'If I told you you wouldn't believe me.'

17

Wesley invited me back to his place for a meal, promising West Indian cooking. His house was in Haberfield, a Federation job on a big block leaving room for a sizeable swimming pool and a garage that had been converted into a gym. Mandy I'd met before briefly. She was small and slight and Wesley would be able to lift her with one hand. Maybe he did. She thanked me for giving them something to cling to about Clinton and her tired smile made me hope like hell that they were clinging to something solid. Clinton, with his narrow, fine features, favoured her.

'Pauline's out busking,' Wesley said. 'Mandy doesn't like it but Pauline enjoys it and says she needs the money. What d'you think about that, Cliff?'

Mandy was watching me. 'I like buskers when they play what I like,' I said.

Wesley took three cans of light beer from the fridge and popped them. 'Diplomatic. You know what I mean. Keeping kids safe. Jesus, our parents hardly had to worry about it.'

I accepted the beer and took a sip. 'Can she handle herself?'

Mandy poured her beer into a glass. 'We've had this discussion a hundred times, even before Clinton . . . '

'Tae Kwon Do,' Wesley said. 'I wouldn't back you against her.'

'Surviving in the city's mostly a matter of confidence,' I said. 'It sounds as if she's got it.'

'Yes, she has,' Mandy said. 'I hope you're right. Dinner in twenty minutes.' She saluted us with her glass and drifted off to the kitchen. I noticed that she held her head rather stiffly and remembered about the whiplash. What you really needed was luck. Confidence wouldn't do you much good when a couple of tons of metal hit you, or some crazy with a gun came wandering your way. Still, it sounded pretty convincing at the time.

Wesley showed me the gym with some pride. 'I've got machines here ain't never been seen. Prototypes, man.'

'For what?'

'Fine-tuning. Show you.'

He showed me by moving massive weights long distances in ways that I didn't really understand, but I grasped enough to see that he'd made significant improvements to the standard equipment.

'Could be money in this,' I said.

Wesley finished the can he'd set aside and towelled off the light sweat he'd raised. 'Yeah, if all this with Clinton gets sorted out I'll think about raising some capital and getting on with it.'

Between the two of them, they'd shown me just how much was riding on my fragile information and hopeful assumptions.

The smoko was set for 10.30 p.m. at an abandoned Mechanics' Institute building in a hamlet near Badgerys Creek that had lost its name along with its population somewhere between the wars, Turkowitz had given me a sketch map which he strongly urged me to eat after memorising it. His little joke. I matched it with some maps I had of the area and formed a pretty good idea of how to get there.

There was nothing to be said in favour of smokos. They were a reaction to many things— the moves by governments to control and perhaps ban boxing, the actions of Mike Tyson in Las Vegas, disappointment at the demise of Fenech and the defeat of Kostya Tszyu. I saw them as a foretaste of things to come if the pressure to ban boxing was successful. Previously, in English-speaking countries, all such efforts had failed and pugilism had survived, usually being conducted under worse conditions than before. I had no doubt that it would be the same again, but the smokos were jumping the gun. There was no protection for the fighters; they were breaking the law and liable to assault charges if discovered. Medical facilities, I'd heard, were minimal, and the equipment was often in poor condition—important when you're talking about the hardness of floors that men might fall down on with force.

I was breaking the law myself by attending and

didn't feel altogether good about it. I had a professional excuse of course, but that wouldn't cut any ice if the cops decided to raid the place. Truth was, I was interested to see what such fights were like because I knew that courage and desperation would be on display and they're always interesting to witness. But I didn't kid myself—the reason smokos existed was not, as their defenders said, to give outlets to aggressive young men. The reason was money. Australians are said to be willing to bet on anything. They'd certainly bet on two men prepared to fight almost to the death. According to all accounts, a lot of money changed hands at a smoko.

The arrangement had been for Wesley and me to go together but he rang me late in the afternoon to tell me that he couldn't make it. Mandy had been taken to hospital with a complication to do with her neck injury.

'She's paralysed,' Wesley said.

'Jesus. What're they saying?'

'What they always fucking say—wait and see. I'm at the hospital now and I've got to stay here. I'm sorry, man.'

'It doesn't matter,' I said. 'You stay there and do what you can. Is your daughter there?'

'Yeah, I wish . . . '

'I know, Wes.'

'You take care, Cliff. There's some mean bastards at those things and some heavy stuff goes down. You can't trust Tank not to double-cross you. And look what happened to that Alessio kid.'

'I'm not a kid. All I'm going to do is identify him and follow him to somewhere I can catch up with him when it suits me. I'll be right. You take care of Mandy. I'll be in touch.'

In one way, I was relieved. It's hard to be inconspicuous in the company of Wesley Scott, and if I was going to be able to play this thing the way I wanted, that's how I'd need to be.

The day had been hot but the Sydney evening breezes were doing their job when I set off for the west. I was wearing jeans, sneakers and a black T-shirt with my freshly washed bush shirt loose over it. The cosh was coiled in my hip pocket; the Smith & Wesson was in the glove box. I had a couple of hundred dollars in cash to bet with and the car was full of petrol. I bought six cans of VB so that I could swing them from a finger by the plastic strapping. Makes a handy weapon that, even if you're forced to drink two or three of the cans beforehand.

You have to wonder what the local cops thought about a procession of cars crawling along dirt roads to nowhere late at night. A football club barbecue? A Vietnam veterans' reunion? A republican movement convention? Surely not an illegal prize fight, not in this day and age. In the old days, when first bareknuckle and then glove fighting were outlawed, the organisers took great care to do two things—first, pick an out-of-the-way spot for the fight and advertise only among 'the Fancy'. Second, ensure that for one reason or another the local constabulary turned a blind eye.

It wasn't unknown for the district magistrate to referee the stoush.

It wasn't a crush, but there was certainly more traffic than you'd expect for that neck of the woods and I noticed a few iridescent markers on the trees here and there just in case we got lost. Not much chance of that. I found myself following a white Mercedes with the vanity numberplate CHAMP. Whoever the champ was, he clearly knew the way, even though his erratic driving suggested that he might have started celebrating something a trifle early. I swigged from a can as I drove just to get into the spirit of things.

The Merc driver flashed his high beam at a dark spot and I saw the light glance off chrome and duco somewhere ahead. Another few minutes brought us into a clearing behind a long, narrow brick building with an iron roof. I could hear a generator humming and there were lights showing in the building and under a big marquee strung between it and some trees. I switched off the engine and my lights, grabbed the cans and opened the door.

A large figure loomed up out of the dark and gripped the door, holding me half in and half out of the car.

'Evening, sir.'

'Evening.'

'Password, please.'

It had slipped my mind. What the hell was it? I was wondering whether I was going to have to grease a palm or two when it came to me. 'Rust,' I said.

'Very good, sir. Please leave the beer in the car. You can buy drinks inside.'

So much for my improvised nulla. Tall and wide, he strode off to intercept the next arrival. I locked the car and went towards the marquee where a bar had been set up, if you call a couple of trestle tables with a keg of beer, an array of bottles, plastic cups and some buckets of ice a bar. About thirty men and five or six women stood around drinking. Most of them were smoking, an unusual sight in a group that size. Twenty-five dollars bought me an admission ticket and another five bought me a can of beer. At those prices the organisers were going to make money whatever happened inside.

I sipped the beer and surveyed my fellow aficionados. The men came in all shapes and sizes but were much of an age, forty and over. Some were in suits, some were as casual as me but there was no one in stubbies and thongs. The word you'd use to generalise was prosperous, or nearly so. The women came in only one category— young, thin and good-looking. They were fashionably and expensively dressed and most of them were showing some gold somewhere. Their companions wore suits and were drinking spirits. Most of the women had champagne. The best-looking of them all was a tall redhead in a tight, short green silk dress with a black jacket. Her partner was twice her age, fat and bald. She had to bend over to talk to him.

His mobile phone rang. He answered it and turned away from her to talk. She caught me looking at her and smiled. There was a lot of promise in that smile, but before I could return it Fatty was snapping his fingers at her and handing her the phone. I moved away so I could watch them from another angle. She finished with the phone and gave it back. Fatty was putting it away when a man who looked something like the attendant who'd met me appeared at his side and spoke to him. Fatty, a foot shorter, nodded, switched off the phone and handed it over. He was given a ticket. It looked like security was tight. Lucky they didn't frisk me and find the cosh.

More cars arrived, more drinks were bought and people began to move into the building. Just out of curiosity, I wondered who Champ was. All I could tell from behind was that he was big with square shoulders and wearing light clothes. I settled on a 190-centimetre heavyweight in a cream suit who was smoking a cigar and trying to make some time with the redhead. Fatty was looking worried but not about the woman. His hand strayed to his belt where presumably he usually kept his mobile phone. Then he remembered and looked annoyed. Workaholic.

I finished the beer, dumped the can in a rubbish bin and went inside. A ring was set up in the middle of the space with rows of plastic chairs on all sides. I estimated there was seating for about two hundred people and the chairs were filling up fast, first come first served. I got on the aisle, giving me a good view, although I was a fair way back. Fatty, the redhead and the man I'd decided was the Champ, sat in front of me. I could always admire her shapely neck and the back of her head if I got bored by the fights. The smoke was thick and getting thicker, it was no place for the respiratorially challenged.

A batch of large, athletic attendants appeared and began handing out sheets detailing the night's entertainment. There were five fights only, two four-rounders, two six-rounders and a main event described as a 'KO contest'—only to be concluded by one of the fighters being unable to continue. The weight divisions were ignored in favour of 'catch weights', meaning that lightweights could be fighting middleweights and middleweights heavyweights and everything in between. The preliminaries were glove fights, the main event was almost a throwback to the nineteenth century—the fighters would have taped hands but no gloves. It was all totally illegal and I could understand the rigmarole of the password, the ban on mobile phones and the breadth of shoulder on the attendants.

In the old days, betting on the fights was an impromptu business organised by the spectators themselves. Not so here. Before the first fight the attendants worked the aisles, accepting and rejecting bets proposed by the punters. The fight card showed how many smokos the fighters had participated in and their win/loss record. Just to be in the swim, I bet ten dollars on Mario (no surnames were given), in the red corner to beat Paddy in the blue at even money. The redhead bet on Paddy with some of Fatty's money.

The preliminaries were unremarkable except for the lack of skill of the fighters, the ruthless urging of their seconds, the laxity of the referee and the bloodlust and ignorance of the crowd. None of the fights went the distance and most of them would have been stopped earlier due to blatant fouls—eye gouging, low blows and use of the elbows—in a legitimate contest. The referee's job seemed to be limited to seeing that the fighters didn't kick each other in the balls and the seconds didn't belt their man's opponent with the stool.

The attendants took orders for drinks and delivered them and most of the crowd was pretty well stoked by the time of the main event. Fatty had slipped out, maybe to drain the dragon, and the Champ had his hand up under the redhead's dress—not a very hard thing to do. I'd lost both bets and was disinclined to throw more money away. It was hard to tell in mayhem like this, but I had a distinct feeling that the results had been orchestrated well in advance of the event. I got another beer and settled back to watch what was the business end of the evening for the fighters, the punters and especially for me.

18

Tank Turkowitz appeared at ringside with his fighter, who was named Kito, and a couple of handlers. Kito was a Maori heavyweight, liberally tattooed and decked out in very flashy boxing gear—tasselled boots, knee-high socks, silk shorts, satin robe. His opponent was Albie, a pale freckled character with wide shoulders and stick-thin legs. When he took off his towelling robe you could see the good muscle definition in his arms and on his chest, but he had to be giving away twenty kilos and fifteen centimetres. He wore plain black boots without socks, black shorts and his taped hands were big, out of proportion to the rest of him. Kito looked to be in his twenties; Albie was thirty if he was a day, with a battered face and going thin on top.

The redhead laughed when she saw him move to the centre of the ring. 'I could beat him,' she said.

I noted Albie's economy of movement, good balance and battle-scarred face and doubted it. Albie had only two attendants, a middle-aged, fortyish man with a hawk face and a hard body, probably Stan Morris, and an Aborigine who was almost as big as Kito. He had a flattened nose, an earring and dreadlocks. He tried to keep his belly pulled in but it was getting away from him fast.

According to the card, Kito had had ten fights for ten wins. Albie's record was eight fights, six wins, a loss and a draw, but if he hadn't had at least fifty fights in the legitimate ring and some in the tents I was no judge. I signalled to an attendant and put fifty dollars on Albie to win inside five rounds. I got odds of three to one and was happy. The redhead turned to look and listen.

'You think that ugly bugger'll win?' she said to me.

'I do.'

'Huh. The strong, silent type. Okay, I say the coconut'll cream him.'

She laughed at her own joke and so did Champ. Fatty, who was back in his seat, didn't react. I thought it was worth a smile.

'I'm betting a hundred on the coconut.'

I shrugged. 'It's your money.'

She giggled. Fatty turned and the look he gave me wasn't a pleasant sight, but he forked over the money. Champ lit a cigar and added to the fug.

The hall had a wooden floor and there was possibly some light padding under the ring canvas, but it couldn't have been much. The canvas was old and stained with blood and sweat. The ropes were frayed where they met the posts and sagged in the middle of each section. No money spent on frills here. The only touch of glamour was provided by the blonde who held up the card to signal the beginning of round one. She wore pasties over her nipples, a g-string and very high heels. She attempted to kiss everyone in the ring except Albie. Kito gave her bum a good feel. That didn't go down too well with some of the less racially tolerant punters.

In the first round nothing much happened. Kito swung and Albie ducked. That was about all you could say. The crowd was unhappy and only Morris and the big Aborigine in Albie's corner looked reasonably satisfied. Albie had no expression at all, just a blank stare over a mouthguard that looked to be too big for him. In the second round Kito connected with a wild swing and Albie shrugged it off and hit him hard in the guts. Kito sagged and Albie waded in, throwing punches. Kito survived the attack and I knew why, even if the screaming crowd didn't. Albie pulled every punch he threw.

Kito certainly was unaware of this and came out in the third with his guard down, swinging from the hip. Albie jabbed him into total confusion, throwing him off balance. Near the end of the round Kito caught Albie in a clinch. This was the only thing I was worried about. The referee would probably have let Kito use his knees, thumbs and head but Albie had the answers. He pounded the Maori's kidneys with bruising short punches that had him gasping for breath and backing away. At that point I was sure Albie could have knocked Kito out and, again, he made a show of it by swinging and upper-cutting. It looked good but the punches mostly landed on Kito's well-padded shoulders. In a nice flourish in the last seconds, Albie turned his opponent like a bullfighter with a bull and then had to steer him back to the right corner. Enraged, Kito swung and landed a heavy punch on the half-turned-away Albie well after the bell. Albie sagged to one knee. The crowd roared. The referee did nothing. The Aborigine jumped into the ring and dragged Albie to the stool.

Tank Turkowitz leaned forward from his seat to talk to Kito's corner man. Both looked happy.

The redhead turned around in my direction. 'Last chance for you.'

I nodded. I was surprised that she could count. The noise level was high and most of the crowd was drunk and watching the blonde. I saw Champ place a bet on Albie to finish inside two rounds. He got better odds than I had and I began to worry that the fix was in. Morris and the other second worked hard on their man—smelling salts, a water spray, slaps and the water bottle. Harry Grebb, one of the wildest fighters who ever lived, used to swig French champagne between rounds. I doubted that was what Albie was getting, but it was bound to be an illegal stimulant of some kind.

Despite all that, Albie looked shaky when he came out for the fourth. His thin legs wobbled and his probing left looked ineffective as Kito lumbered forward ready to let go a haymaker. It was all a fake. Kito's swing missed and Albie hit him right on the button with a left hook that couldn't have travelled twenty centimetres. The Maori's head had continued moving forward and it stopped abruptly. His brain would have bounced against his skull and the blood supply been cut off. He was unconscious before he went down, and the impact of the back of his head against the thinly padded floor would have intensified the concussion.

The crowd screamed. Tank Turkowitz yelled for his man to get up and the corner boys did the same. The referee waved Albie to a neutral corner, the first time this nicety had been observed, and slowly bent over the comatose fighter. He raised his arm and the count he gave must have extended to at least twenty seconds. It was no use. Kito had met his first defeat. The redhead had lost Fatty's money and Champ and I had won.

I collected my winnings and kept a close eye on Albie and his entourage. They disappeared into a changing room at the back of the hall and I hung around outside waiting for them to emerge. The grog was still flowing but I passed. The redhead had got hold of a bottle of champagne and looked set to drink the lot. Fatty and Champ were arguing over something, possibly her. I kept out of sight as Turkowitz and the others bustled Kito into a car. He still looked shaky and I hoped they were taking him to a hospital. Unlikely.

The crowd was thinning and I was beginning to feel conspicuous, alone and sober, when Albie emerged with his handlers. They passed close to me and I heard Morris address the other man as Bindi as he tossed him the keys. Albie was wearing an old tracksuit and sneakers and moved with the same ease he'd shown in the ring. You would have said he was unmarked except that he'd been marked so much so many times before.

Keeping a discreet distance away, I followed them to a silver Tarago parked not far from my car. I noted the licence number and the rip in the cover of the spare wheel at the back. They climbed in and started off, Bindi driving; I let another car get in front of me and fell in behind. Taillights up ahead and headlights behind. The night was over.

It started to rain while we were still on the dirt roads. The rain laid the dust and I took it as a good omen. It's easier to follow someone in the rain—if they have any sense, they pay close attention to the road and drive more slowly. A couple of cowboys passed me, veering close to the trees and the ditch, but the Tarago maintained a sensible speed.

We reached the bitumen and headed towards Sydney. The other cars in front peeled off and I was left to follow the Tarago as carefully as I could. We picked up the Hume Highway in Liverpool and followed it to Bankstown. The traffic was thin at this time of night and I hung back a bit and waited to make the turns. I was equally anxious that the Tarago would get away from me as I was that they'd spot me. Tricky, but it's the only way to do it if you haven't got TV-show things like direction finders and homing devices.

The Tarago pulled up in front of a nondescript

block of flats near the station. Albie climbed out, conferred at the passenger-side window for a minute and then loped off towards the flats.

You'll be somewhere flasher, Stan, I thought as we started up again. *Wonder where Bindi kips?* It was really risky now. The street was dark and long and I couldn't show my lights while we were on the same stretch. I breathed a sigh of relief as the Tarago turned right into a thin stream of traffic. I realised that I hadn't eaten anything for twelve hours and the pangs were strong. Although I had a strong bladder I was feeling a bit of pressure down there and debated whether a can of beer was a good idea. Pissing in the car is never a pleasant experience. The emptiness won and I cracked a can and drank it warm, trying to ignore the bodily signals.

In increasing discomfort, I followed the Tarago up the Concord Road across the river at Rhodes into Ryde. Bindi was a good driver, good in traffic, good positioning on the road. I hung back and it was easier to keep them in sight from a distance in the well-lit streets. The Tarago turned into a road with broad nature strips, big shady trees and houses on big blocks with deep gardens. The house they stopped at was on a bigger than normal corner block where a narrow side street cut in. It was new and two-storeyed with a large expanse of concrete inside a gate that opened by remote control from the car. The gate was set in a high brick fence and floodlights came on when it opened.

I was about sixty or seventy metres back and I

killed my lights as I crawled up closer to get a good look at the place. It was a sure bet Stan wasn't dropping Bindi off here, more likely the reverse, unless Bindi was some kind of live-in minder. He had that look. The Tarago cruised through the gates and I watched them shut behind it. I drew a deep breath, tried to ignore my bladder but couldn't. All I could think of was getting somewhere I could have a piss and quickly. Then I realised I hadn't noted the name of the street. I put the car in gear and was about to move off when the door was pulled open and a hand slammed into the gearstick and made the engine stall.

'Get out!'

It was Bindi. His breath smelled of beer and tobacco and his body smelled of sweat and poor hygiene. He must have moved incredibly quickly to get from where he'd been to where he was now. I started to climb out, simultaneously reaching for the cosh in my pocket. He chopped me hard enough on the side of the neck to half-paralyse me. I lost my grip on the cosh and felt him haul me out, using only one hand. I was a dead weight and a considerable one but it didn't bother him. I got some feeling back as I propped myself up against the car and decided that a kick to the balls was my only hope. He hit me again and that was the end of that. My legs wobbled and my vision blurred. He held me up.

'You followed us,' he grated in the distinctive Aboriginal tone.

'I want to talk to Stan Morris. This was the only way I knew how to find him.'

162

'Yeah, you want to talk, brother? What's the fuckin' blackjack for?'

'I saw you and got scared.'

'Bullshit. You did a real dumb thing tonight. You forget all about it, right? You forget the van, the house, me, Stan, everything? Right?'

I nodded. 'Okay.'

I didn't see the punch coming but I felt and heard my jaw break as it landed. I was blacking out. Then there was a terrible pain in my side as I fell with my full weight against the kerb. I curled myself up, waiting for the kick that would finish me off. The act of curling sent waves of pain through me. The last thing I experienced was a warm rush and a feeling of shame as my bladder let go.

19

White sheets, soft lights, firm, narrow bed, polished floor, pale walls, Venetian blinds—all very unfamiliar. I turned my head to look towards the door and wished I hadn't. My neck was rigid and my jaw felt as though a vice had been applied to it and screwed down tight. I tried to keep my head still and roll my body to the left and that hurt just as much. There was heavy strapping around the lower part of my torso and something inside that felt very loose. I was in a hospital sure enough, but I had no idea how I'd got there or how long I'd been in residence. Private room. Quite right, given the amount of health insurance I pay.

I'd been hospitalised often enough to know how things work. I felt around the bedhead for the buzzer to call the nurse and pressed it. While I waited I tested a few things. Vision seemed all right, teeth intact, legs mobile. My nose has been broken so many times that breathing through it is difficult. There was a heavy dressing along the side of my jaw and I knew what that meant. With my jaw wired up, mouth breathing wasn't easy either. I sucked in a deep breath and felt sharp, stabbing pains in my side and wondered how many ribs had been damaged and how badly. Cracked or broken? Still, it could've been worse. It wasn't nearly as bad as being shot. Then I remembered how my bladder had let go and I was embarrassed to think of the state I must have been in when I reached the hospital.

The door opened and a nurse came in. She seemed glad to see me awake if the wide smile on her pretty Asian face was anything to go on. It made me wonder how bad I'd been on arrival. Punctured lung? Cardiac arrest?

'Good morning, Mr Hardy.'

Was it? Of course, light showing around the edges of the blinds. My voice was a thin squeak through my clamped bones and I realised that my mouth was desert dry. 'Good morning, nurse. Would you mind telling me where I am and how I got here?'

She did nursely things to the bed and looked at the chart. 'You're in the Charlesworth Private Hospital.'

'And where's that?'

'In Ryde. You were found in a car parked in the hospital entrance.'

'With a broken jaw and ribs.'

She nodded. 'Your jaw was broken in two places. You have four cracked ribs but none broken. You were having breathing difficulties and they thought you might have a punctured lung, but you don't. They also suspected a cracked vertebra but there isn't, just compression of two vertebrae which is bad enough.'

'Good news,' I wheezed. 'I . . . ah, must have been a mess.'

'I wasn't on duty. I gather your clothes have been sent to the laundry. Would you like some water?'

'Please.'

She poured water into a glass from a covered jug and inserted a straw. I tried to struggle up and gasped with the pain. She put a cool hand on my forehead.

'Stay there. You can use the straw.'

The water I sucked up tasted better than a cold beer on a hot day. But somehow the drink and the relief it afforded caused me to lose concentration. My eyes fluttered and I saw the nurse move away. I wanted to stop her. I had more questions, but I couldn't summon the energy to speak. All the shapes I could see and everything I could feel seemed to soften and I felt the dope they must have given me kick in and I floated away.

When I woke up again the attractive Asian nurse had been replaced by an older woman and a concerned-looking man in a suit. I kept my head very still but I moved my arms and legs, just to make sure I still could.

'Mr Hardy, I'm Matron Costello and this is Mr Barnes, the administrator of the hospital.'

'Forgive me for not shaking hands.' It would have worked better if it hadn't come out all squeaky.

The Matron gave a thin smile and consulted the chart. I've looked at charts like that myself and they never seem to convey anything, but she looked satisfied.

'You're responding well. Do you feel up to answering a few questions from Mr Barnes?'

'If he'll answer a few from me.'

She didn't like that much but she let it pass and went off to be bossy somewhere else. Mr Barnes drew up a chair, checked his watch, clicked a pen and held it over his clipboard.

'I have to decide whether or not to report the assault you obviously suffered to the police.'

'You won't believe an accident?'

'Certainly not. But Dr Sangster has prevailed upon me to talk to you first.'

It transpired that they'd gone through my wallet when they collected me and found the card that tells anyone finding me in distress to contact Dr Ian Sangster. Ian had come himself and okayed a surgeon to do the wiring and strapping. He'd advised them not to contact the police without talking to me first. Ian can be very persuasive when he tries.

'We saw your investigator's licence,' Barnes said. 'And assumed this has something to do with your profession.'

'Something,' I said. 'I would prefer you don't tell the police. I need to pursue this in my own way.'

'Very well. Not for a while, I'm afraid. You've been quite badly hurt.'

'I'm grateful for the attention I've had. I guess they found my health insurance card, too?'

Barnes scribbled a few words and smiled.

'You're fully covered. I'll hand you back to Matron.'

'I'd prefer the Asian nurse.'

'That was hours ago. She's gone off duty.'

'Can you tell me where my car is?'

'It's in the hospital grounds, locked up and safe. Do you want something from it?'

I doubted that they'd let me have the beer and I hoped I wouldn't need the cosh or the gun. 'No, I just wondered. Will you charge me for parking?'

'You really shouldn't talk so much, Mr Hardy. It can't be easy. I just have a few things here for you to sign.'

I signed and he went away. The Matron came back and asked me if I was in pain. I was and told her so.

'I'm not surprised. You have a wire connecting the hinge of your jaw to the bone. You should by rights be wearing a neck brace, but Dr Sangster said you would refuse.'

'He was right.'

'Pills in an hour,' she said.

'I'd like something to read then, to take my mind off the agony.'

A nurse came in with the day's paper and a couple of magazines. There was nothing new: unemployment wouldn't go down, Australian tennis players still weren't making it past the semi-finals and the cure for cancer was just around the corner. The magazines were full of gossipy stories about models, rock singers and film stars I'd never heard of. The pills arrived with some churned-up muck they told me would be good for me. I felt like a steak and chips and said so. The nurse laughed. I took the pills, swallowed as much of the muck as I could and went back to sleep.

The next day I phoned Wesley and he visited and told me I was an idiot for getting so close to such a dangerous man. I concurred. Mandy was on the improve from a pinched nerve and a consequent panic attack. We agreed to take the matter further when I'd recovered. He smuggled in a flask of Scotch which I drank with water, incurring the wrath of the Matron when a nurse found the bottle.

I phoned Clive, the taxi driver, and told him where I was. He said he'd watch the house and collect the mail, again. He visited a few hours later, saying he'd had a fare in the area but I suspected he was just showing how much he liked me. The Matron and I were now enemies after my infringement. She wore a cross around her neck. I didn't notice this until she asked me if I'd like to see the chaplain.

'Not only do I not want to see him,' I said, 'if he puts a foot inside this door I'll sue the hospital for violating my religious faith.'

Despite herself, she was intrigued. 'And what faith is that?'

'Absolutely none,' I said.

Ian Sangster turned up very early the next morning, reeking of tobacco and the three cups of strong black coffee he uses to start his motor. He inspected his colleague's handiwork and nodded with satisfaction.

'Not bad,' he said, 'for a young feller. Thank you, Clifford, for giving a tyro a chance to improve on his skills.'

'Fuck you. When can I get all this junk off my face and live a normal life?'

'When did you ever lead a normal life? You'd die of boredom after a week of it. You were really pretty lucky, especially with the vertebrae. Oh, I'd say, you could take solids in a couple of weeks. Tough guy like you won't worry about a few cracked ribs, eh? You can walk about a bit this arvo if you feel up to it. I'll prescribe some steroids to help with the mending process.'

'What?'

He explained that steroids had a legitimate role in helping tissue and bones to heal, especially after surgery, as long as the doses were correct and the medication properly produced. I asked him what he thought about athletes using black-market steroids.

'Fine, if you don't mind your balls shrinking and your hair falling out. Don't worry, mate, this stuff won't compromise your manhood.'

'What about women using them?'

He shook his head, felt for a cigarette and remembered where he was. 'More delicate hormonal balance. Women do actually produce some testosterone, but stick in some more, especially the sort of adulterated crap you're talking about, and you're just asking for trouble.'

Ian had brought in a couple of novels but my ribs were so sore and my neck so stiff that I found it hard to get into a reading position. So I lay there and thought. Not to a lot of purpose. As usual, more questions than answers. It must have been Bindi who drove me to the hospital. Why? And one thing was for sure; Stan Morris' very accomplished smoko brawler Albie wasn't on steroids. What did that mean?

The Asian nurse whose name I'd found out was Rose put her head around the door. 'Are you up to another visitor, Mr Hardy?'

'Male or female?'

'Very male.'

'Show him in.'

The door closed then opened and a big body filled the space. I blinked in surprise as he strode towards the bed, dreadlocks swinging. Bindi.

20

Reacting slowly, I fumbled for the buzzer. He was too quick for me and his big hand closed on it before I could find it. I was scared. He was large and powerful and disposed to violence and I was incapacitated.

He moved the buzzer away and released it. 'I guess you don't recognise me, Mr Hardy.'

I tried to get some volume in my voice but it still came out thin and strained. 'Your name's Bindi and you worked me over a couple of nights ago. What the hell are you doing here? Come to finish the job?'

He shook his head slowly and the dreadlocks danced. When he spoke there was no trace of the gruff Aboriginal tone. 'I'm Clinton Scott.'

My jaw would have dropped if it hadn't been wired up. I stared at him. He was clean-shaven now, unlike the other night when he'd had thick stubble. His breath was clean and he'd washed. I tried to imagine him without the flattened nose, chipped teeth, a couple missing, and battered mouth. There was a scar running down the side of his face and he carried an extra twenty kilos. I could almost do it. The fat distorted his features and the belly widened and shortened him. It was difficult to see him as the whip-like young man in the football jumper, but still . . .

'You came to my dad's gym and I took you through your program. Eight minutes stretching, seated bench press, three by twelve reps on . . . '

'Jesus. You *are* Clinton.'

He pulled up a chair. 'That's right. I'm sorry about this.' His hand sketched the work on my jaw. 'I didn't mean to hit you that hard. You sort of leaned into it. They tell me you've got cracked ribs. I didn't do that too, did I?'

'Only indirectly. Your parents . . . '

'Yeah, okay. I can imagine. But I had to do it this way. What the hell are *you* doing? Stan told me to turn you into a vegetable and I told him I had. I'm taking a big risk coming here.'

We talked for an hour. He told me that he'd recognised me, assumed I was looking for him and felt he couldn't let that happen. He apologised again for not doing a better job of pulling his punches. I told him what game I was in and what I'd been doing and he confirmed most of my assumptions. He'd taken up drinking and eating junk food to put on weight. He'd deliberately provoked the fight in Bingara to incur damage to his face. He'd connived with Stella Nickless to get the ransom money. His share was fifteen thousand which he was using to finance his pursuit of the supplier of steroids to Angela.

'I tracked you to Queensland and I sort of thought you'd given that up for a bit,' I said.

173

'You're pretty good at detecting, but you're wrong there. I really got into the Aboriginal thing. I thought it'd get me closer to Angela's spirit. Didn't.'

He'd said he'd learned all he could about Aboriginal manners and mores in order to pass himself off as one as a good disguise when he got back to Sydney and went looking for his revenge. It succeeded. He'd got on to Stan Morris through a footballer who was suffering kidney failure as a result of using steroids.

I said, 'That figures. I talked to Tommy at the Aboriginal settlement out in the Daintree reserve. He said you were interested in payback.'

'You can hardly talk. Want some water?'

He gave me some water, his way of heading off the question, but I wasn't going to be headed off.

'That's dumb,' I said. 'You could go to gaol for twenty years.'

'I don't care,' he said sullenly. 'That bastard killed the most beautiful person on this fucking planet and he deserves to die.'

'Well, if it's Stan Morris and you're so bloody close to him why haven't you done it by now?'

'I nearly did. I sort of wormed my way into his confidence. I fought in one of his bloody smokos and did all right, but I said it was a mug's game and was there anything else I could do. He took me on as a minder and driver and that. He reckons he's one sixteenth Aboriginal himself and that we have to stick together. He offered me some of the shit and that's when I nearly broke his neck. But it turns out he only supplies Sydney.

The guy who supplies the west is a mate of his and they're meeting up soon. When they do, I'm going to kill him and tell Stan why.'

'Listen, Clinton, there's a lot of feeling against all this doping of athletes, especially with the Olympics coming up. If you can get the goods on the suppliers they could go away for a long time.'

Clinton sneered at me. 'Bullshit. Stan makes a ton of money out of drugs and gambling and his mate's probably doing the same. They'd get a high price lawyer and either beat the charge or get it knocked down. How'd I go as a chief prosecution witness, eh?'

Despite myself, I looked at him as he wanted me to. He was right, he couldn't pass as a solid citizen.

'Besides,' he went on. 'If I show up Rex Nickless'll put some heavies onto me. He's done it before, Stella says.'

That was news, but an estranged wife isn't necessarily a reliable witness as I knew from personal experience. 'He says he just wants a statement from you about his wife's screwing him out of fifty grand. He needs it as a leverage in the divorce action.'

'Believe that and you'll believe anything.'

I could see his point but what he was proposing was just youthful madness, inspired by grief rather than logic. 'So what's your plan?'

'After I deal with them, I'll clean myself up. Lose all this flab and get my nose fixed. I'll square things with Mum and Dad and go down to Melbourne and try to get into an AFL side and make some money.'

175

As a mixture of fact and fantasy that took some beating. 'So you'll be Clinton Scott again when you're starring with . . . ' I pulled the only AFL team name I knew from some recess of memory, 'Essendon, and Rex Nickless won't pick up on that?'

'He'll cool down. Hey, I'll pay him back.'

Despite the dreads and the earrings and the flab and the destruction of his good looks, he was a boy again. A very confused boy and one trying to play a part in a man's game. There was the question of who killed Mark Alessio to consider, if that's what happened. But I didn't want to serve that up to him just yet. I tried another tack.

'Look, Clinton, you're not an Aboriginal warrior caught up in some primitive ritual the fucking clever men devised to keep the young bloods in their place. You know about that, don't you?'

'No.'

'That's what a lot of Aboriginal custom was about—old blokes securing the young women for themselves and keeping the young fellers busy elsewhere.'

'I don't believe you.'

I shrugged, which hurt, but I managed it. 'Suit yourself. But anyway, you're a tertiary-educated city man who's as much European as anything else. Your dad's got a lot of Portuguese in him and your mother . . . '

'Stop it! I don't want to hear this shit!'

'You'd better listen, son. Mark Alessio got too close to the action you're talking about and look what happened to him.'

He said nothing.

176

'Maybe *you* killed him. He was in love with Angela, too. Maybe he got on to Stan and you did the job on him with the Tarago.'

'No! No!'

He was upset, close to tears.

'Listen, Clinton,' I said with as much conviction as I could put into my strained voice. 'You're not a desperado. A bit of faked kidnapping and extortion and a touch of standover work is a million miles from what you're contemplating. Give it up.'

'And do what?' he said fiercely. 'You admit you're working for Nickless.'

'And your father.'

'So you say. You're fucking with my mind.'

'Listen, any of those people you've met and admired'd tell you the same—Angela's father, Danny Roberts, Old Tommy . . . '

The pretty nurse opened the door and took a tentative step inside. 'I heard voices raised. Is everything all right, Mr Hardy?'

I looked Clinton in the eye and said everything was all right.

'Pills in half an hour,' she said. 'And you should get some more rest.'

'Fine. I will.'

She retreated. 'Pretty girl,' I said.

He'd noticed but it was the wrong thing to say. He stiffened in his chair. 'You just don't fucking understand.' Suddenly, he reverted to the Aboriginal voice. 'I loved Angela more than you can imagine with your flash Falcon and your lead-weighted blackjack. Let me tell you something, you white bastard . . . '

177

'Why did you come here, Clinton?'

'Bugger you!' He stood up and the bulk of him and the passion in him were frightening. 'I can't sleep for thinking about what happened to her and I'm going to make those fuckers pay, and anyone who gets in my way's going to get hurt.'

I thought quickly and came up with a lie. 'Well, it won't be me. They reckon I'll be in here for a week at least.'

'That'll be long enough. Just keep right out of it.'

'What about your father?' I said quietly. 'He's been helping me.'

'I said anyone!' He threw the chair against the wall and stomped out of the room.

21

The hospital had a balcony running around three sides. The private rooms had French windows letting out onto it. I got out of bed and walked gingerly to the window. Just undoing the catch put a strain on my side and made me wince. I forgot about my trussed-up jaw and swore and that hurt as well. Out on the balcony I sucked in the warm air and moved along and around one side of the building until I could see the hospital car park. I saw Clinton almost jogging towards the Tarago. He got in and drove off, burning rubber.

It was good to be breathing fresh air again and I lingered on the balcony. There was a good view back towards the river and I remembered some good times I'd had in the picnic grounds there with Helen Broadway years ago—salad rolls, white wine and grappling under the trees. I could smell the smoke from her one-a-day unfiltered Gitane and I missed her.

'Mr Hardy! *What* are you doing?'

The Matron was standing by the French window looking as if she'd like to throw me over the balcony.

'Taking the air,' I said. 'Wondering when I'll get parole.'

'You're not a prisoner, you know.'

'Right.' I walked towards her with as much freedom of movement as I could muster. 'And I think I'm going to have to leave. I've got things to do.'

She shook her head. 'Back to bed. Dr Sangster says when you'll leave.'

I stood my ground. 'No, Matron. I'm leaving now. Just bring me the ten or twelve forms I have to fill out and I'll be on my way. I'll need my clothes, of course.'

For a minute I thought she was going to use that admission as her leverage, but she relented, probably glad to see me go after the Scotch incident and my refusal to see the chaplain. After a few minutes my washed and pressed clothes arrived together with my wallet and car keys, shoes and socks. I dressed with difficulty and made my way down to the front desk where I answered questions and signed forms that seemed to waive all responsibility for everything and authorised my medical fund to open the vaults.

'Thank you,' I said to the receptionist as I signed the last form.

Barnes, the administrator, appeared and in-spected the forms. He signed in various places himself and looked at me as if I'd lifted his wallet.

'I think you may find the interior of your car . . . ah, a little offensive.'

'That's okay, Mr Barnes. I'm expecting to find

four cans of beer on the seat. If I don't you've got a pilferer and I'll be displeased.'

He frowned. It wasn't much of a parting shot but the best I could do with my neck, jaw and ribs hurting like hell.

The car was parked partly in the shade, but it must have heated up at times and something of the smell of my urine remained. The beer was on the seat and the cosh was in the glove box but my blood went cold when I saw that my pistol wasn't there. The only explanation for its absence was Clinton and that made me very worried. According to the firearms regulations I was supposed to report the loss of the weapon immediately, and how was I going to do that without screwing everything up? Worrying about it made me almost forget the pain as I drove home. An irrational young man, inexperienced with firearms, in possession of a high-powered weapon and eight rounds of ammunition was a recipe for disaster. And what was I going to tell his father?

The counter on my answering machine told me there'd been six calls. Three of them didn't matter, but three were from Rex Nickless. I checked the office number and found he'd called there the same number of times. On the third call in each case he sounded very testy—more the building site foreman with the hard hat and the rough tongue than the besuited executive. He demanded an update on my activities.

I rang his office and was put straight through.

'Hardy,' he said. 'I got your report and then heard fuck-all. Where've you been?'

'In hospital. I got knocked about.'

'You sound funny.'

'A broken jaw'll do that.'

'Was it Cousins?'

Easy to evade that one. 'Not exactly.'

'Stop pissing me about. I'm still paying you. Have you found him or not?'

'I've spoken with him, yes.'

'Did you tell him what I wanted?'

'He doesn't trust you or me.'

'Who cares? He's in trouble if he doesn't do what I want. Where is he now?'

'I don't know.'

'Jesus! You let him go?'

'Mr Nickless, I was lying in a hospital bed with my jaw wired up and a couple of metres of strapping around my chest. He's six foot two and fourteen or fifteen stone. I wasn't exactly in a position to detain him.'

It's strange how you can visualise the behaviour of a person on the other end of the phone when they're not talking. I suppose it's something you pick up from the breathing, the pauses. I could see Nickless gripping the receiver with whitening knuckles and loosening his silk tie with the other hand as he fought for control over himself. His money usually gave him all the control he needed over other people, except his wife and 'George Cousins'. And me.

'Listen, Hardy, if you're out of hospital you must be okay. Maybe you can't drive. We have to meet.

Tell you what, I'll send someone around to your place to pick you up.'

I thought about that very quickly. 'Okay,' I said. 'Make it in an hour or so. My doctor's coming around in a few minutes to look me over again.'

'Right. I'll see you soon.'

I rang Ian Sangster and told him what I'd done. He swore and said he'd come to see me after his surgery hours. I said I'd be at his place instead, inside fifteen minutes.

'Can you walk?'

'Just.'

Clive's taxi was in the street so I limped next door and asked him for my mail. He was surprised to see me and told me how crook I looked. I thanked him and took the couple of uninteresting-looking letters.

'Did your mate call in?' he asked.

I'd moved away and turned towards the gate, now I turned back and felt pain shoot through my chest.

'What mate?'

'Bloke knocked at the door yesterday as I was going out. Young guy. Tough-looking. Said he was a friend of yours. I told him where you were.'

I didn't like the sound of that, but there was no point in putting Clive on the spot. 'Oh, him, yeah, sure. He dropped in.'

'Right, Cliff. Take it easy.'

Good advice and I'd have been glad to adopt it if I hadn't had at least six things to worry about. The exertion had tired me. I put a banana and some milk in the blender and slowly drank the result. Then I had a large Scotch and drove the short distance to Sangster's surgery.

He smelled my breath. 'I see you've been on the mother's milk.'

I consulted my ancient Swatch. 'This can't take more than thirty minutes.'

'You're going to a disco?'

'Hah.' With difficulty, I stripped off my shirt. Ian removed the strapping, inspected the damage and re-strapped me. He examined my jaw, took my temperature and manipulated my neck. It all hurt but I was stoical.

'Tough guy,' he said. 'You think I don't know what you're suppressing?'

'Look, Ian. I need to be up and doing. I'm taking your fucking steroids and the other bombs you've prescribed. I don't feel too bad, but I need some painkillers that'll cut in quickly and won't make me drowsy.'

He rummaged in a drawer and produced a bottle. 'I can't think how many times I've broken the law in treating you.'

I took the pills and let him help me on with my shirt. 'It adds spice to your life. Thanks, Ian. You've done a great job.'

'You'll live at least until tomorrow. With you, that's about as much as anyone can say.'

'We'll have that drink soon.'

I cracked a can of the warm beer and used it to wash down one of the pills. I drove to a point higher up and one street away where you can observe the area in front of my house if you know how to position yourself. I sipped at the beer and waited with a pair of field glasses finely adjusted to the distance. The pill and the alcohol started to take effect and I was able to perform a few gentle stretches and regulate my breathing.

Eight minutes before the hour I'd stipulated was up, a car stopped outside my house. Blue Camry. I noted the number. Two men got out. They were both big and looked to be in their late twenties or early thirties. Both wore dark suits and ties and one had his hair pulled back into a knot at the back of his head. The other hadn't done anything with his hair except shave it all off. His bald dome glistened in the late afternoon light. They pushed open the gate and advanced towards the front door. I lost them on the overgrown path.

You can't get to the back of the house outside from the front without a machete; the bougain-villea is a knotty, thorny maze between the house and the side fence. I couldn't see these two risking their thousand-dollar suits on that. They re-appeared, conferred, and walked along to the alley a few doors down to take a look at the back. They were doomed to disppointment there as well unless they had a rope and some other shoes in the boot. My back fence is an ordinary, very weathered, paling job, but it sits on top of a two-metre high sandstone wall.

Back they came to the front looking very pissed-off and a bit hot. The blocks in my street are deep and the walk back up the alley is steep-ish. I was untroubled in the shade and wearing a light shirt; walking around in the sun in a suit wouldn't be comfortable. They looked up and down the street, perhaps searching for my car, perhaps because they couldn't think of anything else to do. Baldy leaned against the Camry and lit a cigarette while his mate pulled out a mobile phone and made a call. Then they got back into the car and drove off. They didn't look like draughtsmen or office wallahs who might work for Nickless. They looked like muscle.

22

In response to my phone call, Wesley was at my house in half an hour. He was reassuringly massive in his jeans and sweatshirt. I needed reassurance.

'Mandy's okay,' he said, acknowledging my enquiry. 'What's up?'

'I know where Clinton is. I've seen him and talked to him. He's not rational and you almost wouldn't recognise him physically. He's put on twenty kilos, he's got a busted nose and a flattened mouth and he wears dreadlocks.'

'Who cares? Where is he?'

'He's at a house in Ryde. He's working for a guy named Stan Morris as a standover man.' I touched my jaw. 'He's the one who did this to me.'

'Jesus, it can't be true. He's ... '

'He's been through hell, Wes. He's changed. He fought in one of those smokos they hold in the backblocks. And there's worse.'

'What?'

'He's planning to kill the man who supplied Angela Cousins with the steroids. He's expecting to meet up with him very soon, could be any day.'

Wesley shook his head. Sweat beaded his upper lip and forehead. 'My boy wouldn't kill anyone. Not possible.'

'He's got my gun to do it with.'

That convinced him. 'We've got to go to the police.'

'With what? We've got no grounds to call in the police against Morris. We've got nothing on him.'

Wes acted as if he hadn't heard me. He shook his head and pointed to the phone. 'C'mon, you must have cops you can trust. You can arrange something.'

'I don't and I can't.' My own feelings of guilt about the gun made me testy. 'How about this? D'you want me to get in touch with Nickless and have him accuse Clinton of kidnapping and extortion? We could probably get the cops in on that.'

'No, of course not. Why can't I just turn up there and say it's your father and . . . '

I'd told Wes about his son's masquerade but he seemed to have forgotten. 'Can't do that. He's supposed to be an Aborigine, remember? How'd he explain things to Morris? That'd put him right in the shit.'

'So you're saying we have to do it ourselves? We have to front up to this Morris character and try to get Clinton away from him.'

'Right. Ordinarily, I'd tackle it myself with another pro or two, but I'm somewhat incapacitated. And normally the last thing I'd do is involve a client directly, but I reckon you'd have more influence with Clinton than anyone else on the

188

planet, if we can just get at him properly.'

'Given that Angela Cousins is dead,' Wes said quietly.

'Yeah, that's right. Look, I have to assume Morris has a couple of other guys with him, especially if he's waiting to do a big drug deal. But you must've been in some fights, Wes.'

'Uh huh, very few. You look like this, the drunks and even the racists, they pretty much leave you alone.'

'Must have done your National Service when you were in England.'

He suddenly looked older and sadder, which was not what I was hoping for. 'Yeah, I did it. In Northern Ireland.'

'Perfect,' I said.

I told him about the set-up at Ryde—the size and operation of the gate, the height of the fence, the floodlights, the kind of neighbourhood. He listened intently. It seemed that he'd got rid of all doubt; now he was totally committed. He absorbed the information instantly and I could sense him processing it the way a military field officer does, the way I'd done myself in Malaya but a long time ago and with varying degrees of success.

'Houses next door?'

I racked my brains. I hadn't been planning on anything like this when I'd been there. I hadn't been planning anything and a few minutes later I was in cloud cuckoo land. I tried to visualise the houses on either side and couldn't. All I could see was the trees, then I remembered.

'Corner block. House on the other side much the same as the others in the street. No brick fence. I think.'

'You think. Okay. What about the fence along the open side?'

Open side. Military terminology. Encouraging. I tried, but I couldn't stay with him on it. 'I don't know. Didn't notice.'

'That could be good. You'd probably have noticed something formidable. Right, well, this sounds fairly satisfactory. You see, if this Morris hasn't got any real idea of security or any military experience, he'll assume all you need is something impressive and high-tech out front. That's bullshit. Any piece of territory has points of vulnerability right around the perimeter. Well, I'll ring Mandy and tell her I'll be a bit late. Oh shit, you *are* thinking of doing this tonight, aren't you? You're up to it, are you, Cliff?'

Of course I was. After a couple of Ian's pills and a shot of whisky and with the cosh in my pocket and the illegal Colt .45 automatic I keep for emergencies coming along with me for the ride.

'Sure.'

The night had turned cool, enabling me to wear a light jacket with a pocket big enough to hold the Colt. I gave Wes the directions and we took both cars. The pills helped; I could feel the pain in my side when I shifted gear and turned the wheel but somehow it didn't seem to matter. We drove down the side street and inspected the length of Morris' property. Wes had overestimated

190

my powers of observation—there was a high cyclone fence running from front to back. We stopped further down the street and went into a huddle.

'Depends on the neighbours now,' Wes said. 'He controls the space in front and down that side. He doesn't control the back and the other side. Let's take a look.'

The cyclone fence only ran a metre or so across the back; after that it was a standard paling job.

'Easy,' Wes said. 'Over into the other place and then over the back fence.'

'Wes,' I said. 'I can't scale any fences just now and anyway, I just happen to have a pair of bolt cutters in the car.'

He turned on me angrily, the first sign that he was on edge. 'You've been pissing me about, man. Letting me do the military bit.'

'No. We're going to need all the experience we can muster. You were dead right. This fence is his Achilles heel.'

That soothed him. He grinned. 'I like to work with a man with a classical education.'

'Penguin Classics,' I said.

He chuckled. 'Doesn't matter. Okay, let's check that the fence isn't wired up, which I doubt because any stray dog could set it off, and cut a hole big enough for you to walk through.'

We did that and pushed through a few scruffy casuarinas. I was glad to see Wes hanging on to the bolt cutters as a weapon. That meant he was taking the danger seriously. I showed him the cosh as we crouched in the shrubbery at the side of the house. He nodded sceptically. I didn't show him the gun. It was a while since I'd done this sort of thing and I was nervous. I'd *never* done it with a broken jaw, cracked ribs and stoked up on codeine and alcohol.

'No dogs,' Wes said. 'That's good.'

I hadn't thought about dogs at all. That was *very* good.

The house was brick with a covered verandah running all the way around on the lower level and a deck at the sides on the top storey. At a guess, six bedrooms. There was an in-ground pool at the back, off to one side, balanced on the other side by a sizeable carport. There were lights on in the house and I could hear music playing, or maybe it was from a TV set. We crept around to the carport and found the Tarago and a Holden Commodore of the kind Greg Norman advertises.

As we stood there a car pulled up at the gates and the intercom sounded. A staticky exchanged followed and the gate opened as the floodlights came on. A taxi backed away and a tall, slender woman wearing high heels, a short black skirt and a pink satin blouse strutted towards the house. Her blonde hair bounced on her padded shoulders as she reached into her purse for her mobile phone.

'She'll keep someone busy,' Wes said.

'Yeah. He's so excited he's forgotten to close the gates.'

We both got a better look and Wes said, 'Oh, Jesus.'

She was slender because she was young, very

young. The heavy makeup couldn't disguise the fact. All her movements had a coltish awkwardness, sexually attractive I guess, to some.

She knocked, went into the house and the floodlights died.

'How d'you see it?' Wes said. He was rewarding me for the bolt cutters.

'Two options. We sneak in, try to cut Clinton out somehow, or we do a diversion down here—drive a car into the pool or torch one, something like that.'

'Which d'you favour?'

I stared at the house. I fancied some lights had gone on and others off but I wasn't sure. We had no idea of the layout in there—stairs, doors, lights, furniture.

'Diversion,' I said. 'Chances are it's Morris in the sack. If there's anyone else apart from Clinton we can assume what we like—man, woman, tough, weak, who knows? But Clinton's the muscle. If there's something going on down here, he's supposed to front up.'

'Agreed.'

'I warn you, he's not going to be happy about our interference with his little plan.'

'Bugger his plan. I'm his father.'

I guess that's the way fathers can look at things if they choose. I wouldn't know. There was very little light coming from the house and it was easy to sneak about in the carport, keeping in the shadows. The Commodore was locked. It carried a sign saying that it was protected by a Viper Car Alarm. Wesley pointed to it. I nodded and hunted around in the garage for something to throw. I rejected a screwdriver and a bottle as they are likely to bounce. A hefty shifting spanner seemed like just the thing.

'You realise that this is all as illegal as hell, don't you?' I said.

'So's selling steroids and bashing people up. I'll chuck that thing. With your crook ribs you'd probably miss.'

Call it pride, call it stupidity. I stood back and threw the wrench as hard as I could at the Commodore's windscreen. It shattered and the alarm began to whoop. My ribs protested and my clenched jaw didn't feel good either, but the result was satisfying. Lights came on in the house and the front door opened. Clinton shouted something, jumped from the porch onto the path and ran towards the cars. Despite his bulk, he still moved like an athlete. Wes got ready to intercept him. I got ready to scoot back to the hole in the fence. Everything seemed to be going to plan when the floodlights came on again and a car came roaring through the open gates, heading straight for Clinton and not looking likely to stop.

23

Wes threw himself forward, swept Clinton up and carried him out of the path of the car. It did stop, with a squeal of brakes, throwing a shower of gravel in all directions. Male and female shouts came from the house. The men who jumped from the car, leaving the driver's door open and the motor running, were the two I'd seen at my place earlier. Same car. At night they looked bigger and more threatening. They moved towards where Wesley was holding Clinton in a bear hug. Big as he was and struggling hard, he had no chance against his father's strength.

I pulled out the Colt and got between the heavies and the Scotts. 'Keep out of it, boys. It's a family matter.'

They stopped but didn't look scared. 'It's fucking Hardy,' Baldy shouted above the alarm.

'That's right. Sorry I wasn't at home when you called.'

Ponytail edged closer. 'He won't shoot.'

I shot, aiming well in front of him. More gravel flew, some of it into his face, and he flinched. The Colt makes a sharp report and it brought a scream from the house. Morris appeared on the porch.

'Bindi, what the fuck's going on?' He pointed a remote controller at the Commodore and the whooping stopped.

'Who's Bindi?' Baldy said.

'No-one you know. Get lost.'

The gunshot must have startled and distracted Wes because Clinton broke free of him. He lashed out and caught his father with a glancing blow to the head. Wes reacted more out of surprise probably than from the weight of the punch. He stepped back. Clinton jumped forward and into the Camry. He gunned the motor and shot out through the gate in reverse, swerving, clipping the post as he went.

'Clinton!' Wes shouted, but tyres shrieked and rubber burned and he was gone.

Stan Morris, wearing a silk dressing-gown, came across the gravel, wincing as it bit into his bare feet.

'Will someone tell me what's going on here?' He pointed at me, still holding the gun more or less at the ready. 'You're the fucker who followed us from the fight. Bindi said he'd wiped you off.'

'Not quite, Morris,' I said. 'There's a very long story here and there's been a car alarm and a gunshot. Do we get the cops in or what?'

Wes had walked to the open gate and was staring out at the street.

'Who's he?' Morris said.

'He's the father of the guy you know as Bindi. He's not an Aborigine by the way, he's a West Indian.'

'Shit. And who're these two?'

Without their car and their target, Baldy and Ponytail seemed to be at a loss. I said nothing and waited for the sound of sirens or signs of consternation in the street. Nothing. Maybe the gunshot hadn't been so loud. A backfire. And car alarms go off all the time. Morris' thought processes were running along the same lines.

'No cops,' he said.

'Good,' I said. 'I've got reason to believe you've got illegal substances in there, and if that hooker's sixteen ... '

'Okay, okay. What d'you want?'

Baldy and Ponytail were getting edgy, looking from one to the other. Ponytail felt for his mobile while Baldy lit a cigarette.

'I think you'd better be on your way, boys,' I said. 'You can call yourselves a cab. Just for interest though, how'd you get on to this place?'

Baldy obviously felt a whole lot better with two lungs full of tar. 'We had two cars at your place. You ducked the first one but the second one picked you up and followed you here. Rex is going to want to talk to you, Hardy. We'll deal with the boong later.'

Wes, head bowed, was walking back towards us. I pointed to him with the gun. 'If his father hears you using words like that you'll have to crawl away. Piss off!'

They trooped off towards the gate. Baldy turned around before they got there. 'We know where you live, Hardy.'

'Yeah,' I said, 'and I know what you used to

197

drive. Explain that to Nickless and tell him I'll be in touch.'

The blonde girl was on the porch, smoking and wearing only her pink blouse. Morris shouted at her to go inside. She flicked ash at him but obeyed. Wes advanced on Morris.

'I ought to kill you for using my boy like you have.'

'Hey, hey, he came to me. He looked like a Koori, talked like one and he could fight. How was I to know what he was?'

Wes shook his head and looked at me as I put the gun away. 'I don't know what to do. What'll I tell Mandy? I didn't even get to talk to him.'

Morris' confidence was flowing back. 'I don't think any of this is my fucking problem. You've entered my property illegally somehow. Probably done some damage and . . . '

'Forget it, Morris,' I said. 'You haven't got a legal leg to stand on. Wes, we have to go inside and look at Clinton's things, see if the gun's there and if we can get any idea of where he's gone.'

'You're not going . . . '

Wes took a handful of Morris' dressing-gown at the back and lifted him off the ground with one hand. Morris wasn't light but Wes carried him towards the house with his feet some centimetres off the ground with no apparent effort until the fabric ripped and he fell, skinning his knees on the gravel. He yelped and the blonde girl poked her head out of the door and giggled. Morris shouted an obscenity at her and Wes lifted him up and shook him.

198

'You're a piece of shit, Morris. Go and turn the lights off. And I don't want to see you again, understand?'

Morris nodded and we went up the steps and into the house. The girl had her skirt and shoes on and was unshipping her mobile.

'I'm leaving,' she said.

I nodded. 'Better. Did he pay you?'

'No.'

'Find his wallet and take what you're owed. He won't say anything.'

She was pretty and not yet as tough as she would be in a very short time. 'Right,' she said. Wes started up the stairs and she followed with me bringing up the rear. She went into what was obviously Morris' bedroom and came out flourishing some notes. I escorted her down the stairs and outside in case Morris had turned nasty, but he was standing in the carport looking at his damaged Commodore. The girl gave me a hard, painful tobacco-breath kiss on the cheek, tried for a high five which I couldn't quite get my hand up for, and high-heeled it towards the gate.

I went back into the house and up the stairs. I found Wes in a room at the back. He was looking sadly at his son's meagre possessions: some clothes hung on a metal rack, jeans, T-shirts, a denim jacket—others lay on the floor or on the unmade bed. A few weight-lifting magazines and some newspapers added to the mess. A half-empty bottle of Jack Daniels and a litre-sized bottle of Coca-Cola were on the dressing table.

Beside it there was a paperback copy of Charles Perkins' autobiography, *A Bastard Like Me*, and a brimming ashtray.

'He used to be so neat,' Wes said. 'I kind of worried about it. And he didn't drink or smoke.'

'I didn't tell you about the drinking. I think it started to help him put on weight and disguise himself. The same for the smoking. I don't know about now.'

Wes shook his head sadly, sniffing the strong smell of smoke in the room. 'He moved like Clinton, but he sure didn't look like him. Shit, what a fucking fuck-up.'

There were a few coins on the dressing table and a set of keys, presumably to the Tarago. No notes, no wallet. An op-shop bomber jacket hung on a hook on the back of the door. I felt through its pocket without much optimism. Wes opened some drawers and slammed them shut. There was no sign of the gun. We completed our search and looked at each other. I tried to remember what Clinton was wearing but it wasn't necessary.

'I felt something hard in his jacket when I grabbed him,' Wes said. 'He had on a tracksuit top with zippered pockets. I felt something hard.'

I nodded. The effort of throwing the wrench, the recoil of the Colt, the whole fucked-up business had taken its toll. I reached for the bourbon, uncapped it and took a swig. I handed it to Wes who did the same.

Morris appeared in the doorway. 'What the fuck are you two doing? You're trespassing, you've got no right . . . '

'Where's he gone?' Wes said. 'My son. Where's he gone?'

'How the fuck would I know? Get out of my house.'

Wes advanced on Morris and pulled him into the room. He backed him up against the wall, towering over him. If Morris was an Aborigine he was a pale one and even paler now. Wes looked like a black thunder god, about to send down a lightning bolt.

'You deal in drugs and steroids,' he said quietly. 'You have a confederate who does the same in the western suburbs. He supplied steroids to my boy's girlfriend and she died. He was a good boy, a student at Southwestern University like his girl-friend. Now he's got a gun and the only reason he hung around with you was to meet up with this other scumbag and kill him. Do you under-stand what I'm saying?'

'Jesus, I thought . . . '

'Never mind what you thought. I want the name of this man and where I can find him.'

Morris shook his head determinedly. 'I can't do that. He's a big player. I'm a dead man if I tell you about him. No way!'

Morris' dressing-gown was torn but it was a good quality garment, fastened with a sash. Wes untied the sash and looped it around Morris' neck. 'If you don't tell me I'm going to hang you off the stair rail there. I might drop you and let your neck break or I might just let you strangle to death. That just depends on how quick you are, starting now.'

Morris' eyes bugged from his head with terror.

He could see that Wes was serious, but his nerve held just long enough for one more throw. 'What good would that do? Bindi doesn't know who he is or where to find him. And anyway, he's barking up the wrong tree.'

'Wes . . . ' I said.

'Shut up, Cliff. What d'you mean by that?'

'Bindi . . . your kid . . . whatever the fuck his name is, his girlfriend'd be black, right?'

'Aboriginal,' Wes said.

'Well, this guy, he hates all blacks like poison. He wouldn't have supplied a black chick with anything. No chance. Not in a million years. Slants, yes, blacks, no.'

It was too much for Wes. He slackened the loop and let the sash drop away. Morris gathered himself and pushed past us towards his bedroom.

'Hold on,' I said, following him with Wes drifting off back to Clinton's room. 'You're part-Aboriginal yourself, aren't you?'

Morris smirked as he pulled on a T-shirt and jeans. He rubbed his neck and worked his shoulders. 'Yeah, but see, this guy doesn't know that. But, hey, if Bindi wanted to know who supplies the stuff at that university, I could've told him. Be happy to.'

'Who?' I said.

'Yes, who?'

I turned. It was Clinton, standing just behind me in the passageway and holding my gun pointed straight at Morris.

'Clinton!' Wes' voice was filled with alarm. He didn't forget his military training though, and turned out the light in the room behind him.

'Stay back, Dad!'

'You wouldn't shoot me, son.'

'No. But I'll fucking well shoot Stan if he doesn't tell me what I want to know and I just might shoot Hardy as well for fucking interfering.'

Morris laughed. Despite everything that was wrong with him he had some guts. He came out of the bedroom, turned off the light, and stood in the doorway.

'You're a crazy bastard, Bindi. Sure I'll tell you. Kinnear, Teddy Kinnear. He's the man you want.'

Clinton reached up and smashed the overhead light with the pistol. The area was suddenly completely dark and Clinton was just a rush of fast-moving air as he bolted down the stairs. Wes and I collided as we both went after him and I yelled as my ribs took some of the impact. Wes lost balance and fell on the first stair, tumbling heavily to the landing. Above us in the dark, Stan Morris laughed again.

24

By the time we'd collected ourselves and made it to the front door we knew we were too late. The roar of an engine and the protest of tortured tyres told us that Clinton was away again.

'I can't believe this,' Wes said. 'I had two chances at him and screwed up both times.'

I was rubbing my ribs and feeling for the bottle of pills. I needed them, and the whisky if possible. I yelled to Morris to bring it down. He came down with the bottle and the phone in the passage rang. He answered it as I took a swig.

'Yeah, well you nosy old cunt, I'll tell you what you can do. You can get fucked!'

He slammed the phone down and snatched the bottle from my hand. 'Neighbour—old cunt.'

'So you said. You realise you left the gate open after your playmate arrived.'

Morris wiped the neck of the bottle on his sleeve and drank. 'Shit.'

'He came back to beat information out of you, you know. You're lucky we were here.'

'That's a laugh. I wish I'd never seen you or him and you can get out right now.'

'Just a minute,' Wes said. 'Do you know where this Kinnear lives?'

'Not a fucking clue. Out west somewhere, that's all I know. Look, I'd tell you if I knew. It's nothing to me.'

'I believe him, Wes. Hang on, let me think. I know the name.'

Wes rubbed the slight bruise on his cheek where Clinton's punch had caught him as if it was a way of maintaining contact with his son. I repossessed the bottle and hoped the pain-killers and whisky would stimulate my memory. They didn't. I knew I'd written the name down and I mentally flipped through my notebook.

'Got it! He used to be the university basketball coach. His assistant's taken over. Clinton must know him and he probably knows where he lives.'

'He's irrational.' Wes said. 'He could kill him. We have to stop him.'

Morris was listening, interestedly but unsympathetic. 'You'd better call the cops. But not from here.'

Wes shook his head, 'We can't. Put the police up against an armed black man looking the way he does? That'd be signing his death certificate.'

I caught the last few words as I went through the door. I took the steps as fast as I could and hobbled back towards our hole in the fence. Wes caught me at the carport.

'What the hell are you doing?'

I handed him my keys. 'Just get to the car and get it started.'

He didn't argue. He had the motor running

when I reached the car. I climbed in, said, 'West,' and reached into the glove box for my notebook. I located Kathy Simpson's number and punched it in, hoping she was home.

'This is Kathy.'

'Kathy, this is Cliff Hardy, remember me?'

'Yes, Mr Hardy. How are you?'

'Okay. Now this is terribly important. Have you got an address and telephone number for Ted Kinnear, the old basketball coach?'

'Not here. It'd be at the desk at the gym.'

'Is it still open?'

'Yes, there's a game on tonight.'

'Kathy, this is literally life and death. It's to do with Mark and Clinton and Angela and all that. I have to have that number and address. Can you ring the desk and get it and phone me as soon as you have it. Here's the number.'

She was up to it. 'Just a minute, I'll write it down.'

I gave it to her and tried to think if I'd covered everything. 'Last thing. Have you any idea where he lives.'

'Parramatta,' she said. 'I think, but he's sick and ... '

'Quick as you can, Kathy.' I rang off and let out a slow breath. 'Parramatta, Wes. Somewhere in Parramatta.'

We drove for a while and I felt the codeine and alcohol take effect. I took out the Colt and checked the action.

'I'm glad you didn't pull that out when Clinton was pointing the gun at Morris.'

'I didn't even think of it.'

'Good. Don't!'

I put the gun in the glove box and drummed my fingers on the dashboard. The phone rang and I snatched it up.

'Mr Hardy. I've got what you want.'

She gave me the phone number and address and I thanked her abruptly, rang off and called the number.

'This is Ted Kinnear. I'm not in at the moment but I won't be away long. Leave your name and number and I'll call back.'

'What?' Wes said.

I scrabbled through the dog-eared, broken-spined *Gregory's* for the street. 'Good news. He's out. Gives us some time.'

We drove in silence for a while and I could feel the tension building in Wes. He drove too fast but skilfully and I tried to think ahead to what we might be confronting but there were too many imponderables. I reflected that, like most of the important moments in my life, this one was impossible to plan for and all I could do was play it out by instinct and experience and hope for good luck. I wondered if Wes felt the same and doubted it. He'd plotted his life's moves with shrewd intelligence and, besides, he had a hell of a lot more at stake here than me.

'D'you want to call Mandy, Wes? Give her some idea of what's up?'

'No. I want to be able to tell her that Clinton's with me and he's safe and everything's all right.'

'Okay,' I said but I thought, *I hope to Christ you can do that.*

I phoned Kinnear several times on the drive but got the same message. There seemed to be nothing remarkable about his address—a suburban house in a suburban street. When we arrived there *was* something remarkable, to us at least—a blue Camry parked further down the street. We stopped behind it. There was a scattering of cars parked in the street.

'He's here,' Wes said.

'Yeah, probably inside. Wonder what he made of my phone calls.'

Wes opened the door. 'I've got to go in and talk to him. Make him see sense.'

'Hang on,' I said. 'Look there.'

A station wagon passed us and pulled into the driveway of Kinnear's house. The gate was open and the car drove in and out of sight behind some shrubs. Wes jumped from the car and sprinted towards the house. I grabbed the Colt from the glove box and followed him at the best pace I could muster.

The house was a double-fronted weatherboard with a California bungalow-style wide front porch on a large block. The garden had been carefully tended at one time but had been let go—the grass was long and weeds had invaded the flower beds and were sprouting up around the bases of the shrubs. Wes hesitated at the porch and I caught up with him.

'At the back,' I whispered. 'He'd go from the garage to the back door.'

'Where's Clinton?'

I didn't answer. Instead I got going around the back, hoping to be able to size up the situation before Wes barged into it, charged with emotion and a good chance to get himself shot. We stopped dead when we rounded the back of the house. Lights were blazing in a glassed-in sun porch and we could see two figures, distorted and unclear through the dirty louvres, standing in the middle of the room. Both were tall and heavily built, but it wasn't difficult to pick out Clinton. He was the one with the gun in his hand. The gun was pointing at the middle of Kinnear's chest.

I held Wes back with one hand. 'This is dodgy. That pistol doesn't need much of a pull.'

'God damn you for letting him get it.'

That was helpful. We crept closer to the back door and could hear what was being said inside.

'I know you gave her the steroids, Ted,' Clinton said. 'I fucking know!'

'I didn't, Clint! I swear I didn't.'

I felt Wes react as Clinton swiped Kinnear across the face with the pistol and then had it quickly poised again. 'You're lying.'

Kinnear reeled back under the blow but he didn't fall. It seemed to galvanise and embolden him. 'Well, fuck you, Clint. What if I did? She begged me for the stuff. She knew she wasn't good enough to make the Institute unless she got stronger. I just did what she wanted. You could've done with a dose of the same at the time. You're a fucking fat pig now, but.'

I expected Clinton to hit him again but he

didn't. Instead, still moving with athletic grace, he got behind Kinnear.

'Outside,' he said quietly.

'Why?'

'I'm going to execute you and I'd rather do it outside.'

'You wouldn't.'

'I will. I'll kill you and then myself. And I don't want to die in your filthy fucking house. Move!'

He clouted Kinnear on the side of the head with the pistol. Not hard, but enough to jolt him, then he shoved him ahead. Instinctively, Kinnear pushed the door open and stepped out into the yard. Close behind, Clinton kicked him precisely in the back of the right knee. Kinnear collapsed on the broken cement path. Then Clinton saw us. He didn't hesitate. He moved forward, grabbed Kinnear's collar, jerked his head up and rammed the pistol into the base of his skull.

Wes stood and extended his hand. 'Clinton, don't do it, son. You'll ruin your life for this old . . . '

'Stay there, Dad. My life's over, good as. It just didn't work out.'

'That's crazy. Think of your mother and your sister.'

There wasn't a lot of light in the yard but I could see the tears on Clinton's face. 'All I can think of is Angela and how this bastard killed her.'

It was impossible to tell whether he'd cocked the gun. If he hadn't, it wouldn't fire and we could get to him in the time it'd take him to cock it. But if he had, he could do what he threatened in a matter of seconds.

Kinnear was petrified but he managed to turn his head slightly towards us. 'Do something,' he pleaded.

'They can't,' Clinton said. 'Goodbye, Dad.'

'Clinton. No, boy, no.'

The guttural Aboriginal voice was firm and arresting; Clinton turned to look but kept both hands in place. Joe Cousins and Kathy Simpson stepped into the patch of light coming from the porch.

'He killed Angela, Mr Cousins,' Clinton said. 'He's admitted it.'

'Don't let him kill you then,' Joe Cousins said. 'Give us the gun.'

He moved forward, almost casually and, strangely, Kathy came with him. For no good reason, it struck me that she was the only fair one among us. She seemed to glow in the faint light and she was making murmuring noises of comfort directed towards Clinton and he wavered. It could have been the presence of someone young like himself, or maybe the authority Joe Cousins was exerting or both, but Clinton relaxed his grip on Kinnear's collar and let him sprawl forward. Beside me, Wes relaxed as Cousins took the pistol from Clinton's hand.

'Good boy,' he said. Then he bent, placed the gun to Kinnear's temple, fired and blew the top half of his head away.

25

Clinton moved to grab the gun, probably still intending to kill himself, but his father clipped him with a short right that buckled his knees. Wesley held him. Clinton struggled but then sagged and burst into tears. I took the pistol from Cousins who was standing calmly by. Then both men comforted Clinton as he cried his young heart out.

Kathy Simpson stood with her hands up to her face. She was shaking. I'd taken the gun by the barrel. I laid it down on the steps and put my arm around Kathy's shoulders.

'I'm sorry,' she said. 'I'm sorry. I thought I should bring Mr Cousins. I didn't know what was going to happen.'

'No one did, Kathy. You did the right thing. Mr Cousins stopped Clinton from shooting him.'

'But . . . but Mr Cousins . . . '

'It's better this way,' I said. 'It won't be too bad. I'm going in to phone the police. You come in and sit down, or make some coffee or something. It's a hard thing for a youngster like you to see, but you'll get over it. Just come inside and don't look.'

In fact we all went inside and they sat around

the laminex kitchen table in silence while I phoned the police. Kathy drank a glass of water but didn't make coffee. I doubt that anyone would've drunk it. It wasn't a time for routine gestures.

Joe Cousins was composed and dignified and Wesley had trouble concealing his pleasure and relief. Clinton had calmed down. He sat beside his father, staring straight ahead as if there was something interesting written on the wall. His mouth moved as he muttered something but I couldn't catch what it was.

'I never shot a gun like that before,' Joe Cousins said. 'A hand gun I mean. It's easy isn't it?'

'Yeah,' I said. 'Too easy.'

A police siren sounded and he sat up straighter in his chair with his gnarled boxer and axeman hands clenched in front of him.

'Listen, Joe,' I said. 'Don't say a word to the cops. Don't say a single word until you've got a lawyer right there with you.'

Cousins almost smiled. 'Okay. Yeah. Things've improved that way. We've got some bloody good lawyers now.'

I met two uniformed policemen in the driveway, identified myself and the other parties dead and alive and told them the bare minimum, using the most neutral language I could command. I showed them the body and the gun but refused to say anything about who had done what to whom. The younger of the two cops was inclined to be aggressive but the older one knew the drill. He went into the house and observed the silent foursome sitting around the table.

'Wait for the D's,' he said to his partner. 'Let them handle it. It's not as if we have to chase after anyone, is it, Hardy?'

'No. We're all here. Or nearly all.'

'What the fuck does that mean?'

'It's a long story,' I said.

As soon as the story broke, Rex Nickless rang me to say that he wanted nothing further to do with Clinton or with me. He considered our account closed. I reminded him that there was a Camry sedan belonging to him parked in a Parramatta street.

'You're a bastard, Hardy.'

'How's your wife?' I said.

He laughed. 'We'll work something out.'

'I've also got six thousand dollars of your money that didn't get spent.'

There was a pause and I could imagine him thinking about it, calculating whether it was worth recovering and what my terms might be.

'Use it to defend the Abo,' he said.

Joe Cousins pleaded not guilty to murder on the grounds of diminished responsibility. He was brilliantly defended by a black barrister in front of an all-white jury. Wes and I gave evidence that Kinnear had admitted supplying the steroids that had killed Angela Cousins. Quantities of the stuff were found in his house along with other evidence of drug dealing. Cousins was convicted of manslaughter and sentenced to seven years imprisonment, eligible for parole after three. He declared himself well satisfied with the result.

The death of Mark Alessio remained a mystery. It was possible that he'd found out about Kinnear's involvement and that Kinnear had run him down. Possible, but impossible to prove. The vehicle that had killed him was a station wagon and the police questioned the witness in an effort to establish if Kinnear's station wagon filled the bill. The witness couldn't be sure and forensic examination of the car failed to confirm the suspicion.

For a time, Clinton Scott was a lost soul. Wes and Mandy did all they could for him but something vital in him had been damaged. He made an effort to stop drinking and lose weight but failed. He lost all interest in sports and never came near the gym. I asked Wes about him from time to time and got negative replies until one day he showed me a newspaper photograph of a noticeably slimmer Clinton sitting cross-legged in a group being addressed by a shaven-headed Asian wearing a yellow off-the-shoulder robe.

'What's this?' I said. 'I have to say he looks a lot better.'

Wes shook his head resignedly. 'He's become a vegetarian. He's studying Eastern philosophy.'

'It could be worse.'

'How.'

'Western philosophy.'

I was in trouble myself, of course, for not reporting the loss of my pistol and the consequences that flowed from that. I pleaded incapacity through injury.

I was disqualified. I appealed and the case comes up for a hearing in a couple of weeks. My injuries healed and I tried to settle back into a routine of regular work in the gym, but my resolution wavers. I miss too many sessions too often. Ian Sangster expressed no sympathy when I told him about my lapses.

'What's the point of making a great corpse?' he said, lighting an unfiltered Chesterfield.

I stayed in touch with Kathy Simpson, reassuring her that nothing that had happened that night in Parramatta was her fault. She seemed to accept it eventually. Her graduation comes up about the same time as my licence disqualification hearing.